DYNASTY

III

BY

DUTCH

www.dcbookdiva.com

ISBN-10: 0984611088
ISBN-13: 9780984611089
Library of Congress Control Number: _____

Paperback Edition, February 2013

Publisher's Note

This is a work of fiction. Any names historical events, real people, living and dead, or the locales are intended only to give the fiction a setting in historic reality. Other names, characters, places, businesses and incidents are either the product of the author's imagination or are used fictiously, and their resemblance, if any, to real life counterparts is entirely coincidental.

Edited by: Jenell Talley
Proofing: Marion Dixon Bey
Inside Layout/Typset: Linda Williams

DC Bookdiva Publications
#245 4401-A Connecticut Ave
NW, Washington, DC 20008
www.dcbookdiva.com
facebook.com/dcbfanpage
twitter.com/dcbookdiva

DUTCH

DYNASTY III

DC BOOKDIVA PRESENTS

Dedicated to all our readers who continue to support K.T., he writes from his heart and for the love of his fans.

Enjoy,

DC Bookdiva

CHAPTER 37

Tre hung up and turned to Vee excitedly.

"Yo, fam, we got that bitch-ass nigga!"

"Who?" Vee asked, finishing his beer.

"Remember the hot nigga I told you about? The CI"

Vee's interest perked up.

"Yeah?"

Tre's phone rang with a text.

"My connect just hit me wit' it. It's gonna cost us ten stacks, but shit, it's worth it!"

Tre popped the text, looked at it strangely, then said, "Yo … this name sound familiar."

"Let me see."

He handed the phone to Vee. Vee shielded the screen from the glare of the sun when he saw it. He couldn't believe his eyes.

The text said Guy Simmons.

It couldn't be.

Guy Simmons?

Not Guy Simmons.

Not his father.

Vee didn't want to believe it, but the proof was staring him in the face.

"Yo, who the fuck sent you this? How they know?" Vee questioned Tre intently. He wanted 110% assurance the information was correct.

Tre took back his phone.

"That's my little mole, yo. He ain't never let me down before. Believe me, if he say it, it's official tissue," Tre assured him. Vee looked out at the crowded beach and shook his head.

"What? You know this cat?" Tre inquired.

"The cat I was wit' in New York. His name Guy," Vee replied without looking at Tre.

Tre punched his hand with his fist.

"That's where I heard that name! Goddamn, I'm slippin'. Good thing—"

"But I don't know if his last name Simmons," Vee lied.

He couldn't put his finger on why he said it, he just knew he had to say something. That text had all but signed Guy's death warrant, but something inside Vee granted him a stay of execution, even if it was just to make sure there was no mistake.

"But shit, it could be, yo. Shit, that nigga too close. Fuck, he was there, yo," Tre emphasized, referring to the Sarducci hit. The implication was enormous. Tre meditated murder with weapons of mass destruction, and Guy could name names and give dates. If he was the C.I., this type of information would be gold to the Feds. "Naw, yo, that's some serious shit to put on a muhfucka. Let me handle this," Vee said.

"That's what's up, fam. Do you. I'ma just pour Tito a drink on this—"

Vee cut Tre off sharply, maybe too sharply, and looked at him.

"Naw. I said let me handle it, a'ight? Let this stay between us … for now."

Tre looked at Vee, then shook his head.

"Fam, what up? I mean, who is this dude?"

My father, Vee thought bitterly to himself, but he answered, "A minute ago you said it ain't about trust, but at least don't NOT trust, right?"

Tre weighed every word Vee said. Although he hated snitches, he knew shit was deeper than still waters with the situation. He still hadn't asked Vee about the altercation with Tito's man, or how he knew Tito's man at all. But he felt like Vee would tell him when he was ready.

"Yo, fam, handle it then. Just know, yo, all our lives at stake, so whateva it is—"

"Say no more, yo, I already know. If it is what it is, then it is what it is, feel me? I'll handle the nigga myself," Vee vowed sincerely, knowing in his heart that's the only way it would go down. But make no mistake, if it had to go down, Vee wasn't going to hesitate to kill Guy.

●●●●●●

"Ty," Guy began, trying to wrap his head around everything he had just heard. "Why did you kill his family? When was this?"

Ty was at a loss for words. What could he tell Guy? If he told Guy it had been Brah that had tried to kill him, then Guy would want to know why he hadn't told him so. To tell him that much could lead down a slippery slope to Pandora's Box.

One thing was for sure: Ty could tell from Guy's reaction that he had no idea of the truth, and that thought alone gave him some relief because it meant he had room to maneuver.

"Shit was crazy, Pop. Ere'body was suspect and nobody was gettin' a pass," Ty explained. "A couple of things pointed in Hardy's direction, so we moved on him."

Guy paced the floor. The name Hardy meant one thing to Guy: Brah Hardy.

He looked at Ty.

"Couple of things like what? His uncle Brah?"

Ty's heart bumped, but he kept his composure. He had to switch up the direction of the conversation because it was veering too close to the truth. But before he could, Hawk Bill said, "That might been my father, Guy. When Ty came to me, I told him about Brah just comin' home. Is that what you talkin' about, Ty?"

Hawk Bill offered the information to save Ty, but he was pushing him deeper without even knowing it.

"Naw, that ain't have nothin' to do wit' Kev. He thought the Wolf Pack mighta been usin' Hardy to set you up," Ty told them.

"The Wolf Pack? Guy echoed. "But that didn't make any sense."

"And even if he did think that, how is it y'all killed everybody but Hardy?" Hawk Bill added.

The questions were coming too fast for Ty to handle.

"Look, like I said, shit was crazy. It was a dead end, but I don't regret it. Besides, it was Kev's call and I followed his lead," Ty replied, putting the weight on his dead brother. "Regardless, I don't care nothin' about the Hardys," Ty added, but inside he flinched knowing that in reality he was a Hardy. "All I care about is that nigga killed my mother! So until he dead, that's all I care about."

Guy nodded with understanding.

"We'll find him, no matter where he at."

"And he ain't too far. The boy too dumb to run and he got too much pride to hide. He's around," Hawk Bill surmised.

Guy walked up to Ty and put his hand on Ty's shoulder. He wanted to comfort him, not only for the obvious reasons, but for the not so obvious. His heart grieved for Ty because he had killed his own father without even knowing it.

Or so he thought.

"Ty … I wish you knew how sorry I am about everything. I know how things can get out of hand," Guy offered.

Ty nodded, knowing exactly what Guy was talking about.

He knew Guy was apologizing for him having to kill his own father. A part of him wanted Guy to sit him down and tell him the truth. Then maybe, just maybe, Ty would feel compelled to reciprocate. But he knew everyone had their own secrets and their own reasons for keeping them.

"It is what it is, Pop. She's gone and it's nothing I can do to change that. You all I got now, and I'll be damn if I let anything happen to you."

Guy smiled.

"Same here, youngin'. I love you, son."

"I love you too, Pop."

Guy took a deep breath then withdrew from the moment by turning to Hawk Bill.

"Hawk, find that nigga yesterday."

"No problem"

"And, Ty," Guy added on his way out the door, "I need to speak to Karrin. Maybe something Kev did or said will help us understand this Hardy connection better, you know? Find her and bring her to the house."

"Okay," Ty replied, but he had no intention of doing so.

⚫⚫⚫⚫⚫⚫

Deeper ...

Deeper ...

Twenty years deeper ...

The last time Shantelle had felt all of Guy inside of her she was a young girl with her whole future ahead of her. Now she was pushing 40 and at peace with the past. The one thing that hadn't changed was Guy's ability to curl her toes with his never-ending long stroke. She gasped, "I love you, Daddy."

"I love you too, baby girl," Guy crooned softly in her ear, then ran his tongue along the curve of her neck.

Shantelle let out a soft moan and arched her back, meeting Guy's slow but breathtaking thrust.

She had dreamed of this moment so many times in prison. For years, it was the thought of Guy deep inside her while she touched herself that had put her to sleep at night. Even when she went through her phase of letting another woman eat her out, the thought of Guy's touch kept her from being totally turned out. She longed for his touch even when she thought she hated him.

Shantelle cuffed her leg around Guy's and twisted her body until she was on top of guy grinding her hips in rhythm with his strokes as he moaned with pleasure.

"You like that, daddy, huh?" she groaned.

"I missed you, baby girl," Guy replied, taking her nipple in his mouth and applying the amount of pressure he knew would make her cum again.

Shantelle bit down on her bottom lip and coated Guy's dick for the third time. She began riding him more vigorously, despite the pain, because of the pain, the pleasure of the pain of his massive manhood filling her to the max.

"Give it to me, daddy! Cum in this pussy! Fuck me!" Shantelle cried out in the throes of passion.

Guy gripped her phat ass and spread her cheeks, engorging her womb until she trembled and shook. He trembled and shook and they both came like the rain.

Shantelle collapsed on his chest, panting. She gained her composure, then giggled and said, "Not bad for an old man."

"Old man?" Guy chuckled. "Ain't no way."

They shared a laugh. Shantelle ran her hand along his cheeks, tracing his graying temples. "It looks good on you, though. You wear it well."

Guy smiled, took her hand in his and kissed her fingertips.

"But, Guy …"

"Yeah."

"You don't love me," she said simply, referring to his words voiced in the moment of lust.

"Baby girl, stop playin'. I've always loved you. I know I ... got around but—"

Shantelle put her finger to his lips.

"Shhh ... it's okay. Just like you can't help who you love, you can't help who you don't love either. You didn't love me, you don't love your wife, and you definitely didn't love that ..." Shantelle started to say "that bitch," but decided not to speak ill of Debra because she was dead, so she held her tongue. "You definitely didn't love Debra," she continued. You wanted to possess us, so of course you took care of us."

"Because I wanted to make you happy. I still do," Guy replied.

"But that ain't love, baby. But it's okay, you know? I can deal with that," Shantelle said, peeling herself off of him enough to prop her head up with her hand. She traced his nipple with her other. "And even though I do love you, you gonna have to deal with some things too."

"Like?" Guy arched an eyebrow.

"Like me seeing other people if I so choose. Like me being an independent woman who wants and respects your advice and support, but is capable of making her own decisions," she jeweled him with just a hint of sass.

Guy definitely wasn't used to a woman bringing it to him like that, but he kept his composure.

"And while you seein' these people and makin' decisions, what am I supposed to do?"

"You, like the young folks say, do you, Guy. Life is too short to be waitin' on you to have time for me to give my life meaning, you know? I love you dearly, but I love me too."

Guy smirked. "Baby girl done grown up, huh?"

"Damn skippy," Shantelle retorted, rolling her neck like she used to, then kissing him on the nose.

They shared a laugh between equals.

"You hungry? You want a sandwich or something?" she offered.

"Oh, you still cook for me? I mean, you done all but slapped a skirt on me. I didn't know what to expect," he joked.

Shantelle playfully hit him and sat up. Guy watched her slip on her T-shirt.

"But listen, there's something else I need to talk to you about," Guy began.

Noticing the weight in his tone, Shantelle sat back down.

"What?"

Guy sighed.

"It's about your son. I—"

Shantelle held up her finger, and Guy knew exactly what she was about to say.

"Our son," she corrected.

"Believe me, baby girl, I accept that fully. It's just … he so goddamn hardheaded, and I need you to speak to him. There's an investigation getting started about the Wolf Pack, his crew. It can get serious real quick," Guy explained.

"How serious?" Shantelle questioned, concerned.

"Drugs, murder, maybe even RICO," Guy answered.

Shantelle took a deep breath. She had just done twenty years in a cage, so just the thought of her child facing the same fate gripped her heart. She took a deep breath.

"Then I think you should talk to him, not me. I know he's hardheaded, but look who his parents is," she chuckled to stifle the tears. "Just do what you can."

Guy nodded, then watched her walk out. His heart was heavy with guilt, not because of his absence from Vee's life but because he had been the catalyst that had started the investigation in the first place.

CHAPTER 38

**Six Months Earlier, one week after
the Banks family was murdered**

It was a crime scene detective Mike Franklin would never forget. It was a crime that Durham would never forget. Several victims, including an infant and an elderly person, were each stabbed more than fifty times. It had been a week since the murders, and the smell of pee was overwhelming. It clung to the whole neighborhood like a wool jacket in the summer. The stench was the reason the bodies were found. Like God built in the ability to identify the unjustly slaughtered. It was sadistic and gave new impetus to the war on drugs in Durham.

Franklin was born and raised in the ghetto of east Durham, so he knew how violent the city could be. But this was a face the drug game had never showed him, and it made his mind center on four words: GET THE WOLF PACK.

It hadn't even been a week, and the fact that the Wolf Pack had committed these atrocious acts was common knowledge in the streets. The rumor had been initiated by a small-time hustler named Silk. The same Silk was rotten and hung up.

Silk was a Fed mole. He leaked the Wolf Pack's involvement to the streets and the info took on a life of its own.

Franklin maneuvered his way through the many people at the crime scene. His swagger was an understatement.

Like a hint of cologne, and reminded those who, meeting him for the first time, of Will Smith. He approached Detective Sergeant Allen Randall and shook his hand.

"Detective Franklin, good to see you, just not under these conditions," Allen commented.

"How are you, Sarge?" Franklin returned the greeting.

Franklin liked Randall although his anger was police politics. He wanted to make chief someday. Solving cases was just a means to that end.

"I'm glad the wheel stopped on you for this, Franklin. This is one you don't get every day," Allen remarked and then pulled out his small notepad. "We've got several victims: one elderly female victim and two adults, one female and one male, all stabbed multiple times, some as many as fifty, mainly to the face. Corpses already decomposing bad for forensics. The only lead we have is the neighborhood grapevine. Some drug gang calling themselves the Wolf Pack. "You ever heard of 'em?"

"Unfortunately," Franklin replied. If you were young and black in Durham with any connection whatsoever to the streets, the name Wolf Pack had nothing to do with N.C. State.

"Funny, I never knew these drug guys to get up close and personal like this. They usually use automatic weapons," Allen remarked.

Glancing around at the rotting bodies, Franklin surmised, "This was personal, very personal. Maybe even one of their own."

Allen nodded. "Glad the wheel stopped on you for this. I know we're in good hands," Allen said, shaking his hand.

"Well, it's all yours. This one could be your ticket, Franklin. Maybe even have my job," Allen winked, then walked off.

The comment went in one ear and out the other. All the incentive Franklin needed was laying and rotting all over the floor. He surveyed the scenery, trying to get a feel of what took place. He knew it wouldn't be hard to get the pawns who actually carried out the mission. Franklin wanted the head, the man who ordered the massacre.

"Excuse me," Franklin said to a member of the forensic team who was taking pictures. The guy looked up. "I want a copy of all the victims as soon as possible.

"Sure thing, detective."

Franklin would use those gruesome images as a constant reminder of the monster still on the loose.

As soon as Franklin got back to his office, he went to work. He needed to know all he could about the Banks' family, Banks wasn't a common name in Durham, but neither was it unique. He started his investigation, shifting through several screens of information. He was looking for any known criminals with the last name Banks. He was checking to see if that particular house had been the subject of any disturbances and more importantly, whether it had ever been used as collateral to post bond. If his hunch was correct, that the murders were done against one of the Wolf Pack's own, then he knew the house had been used to post bail.

Fifteen minutes into his research he hit pay dirt.

"Bingo!" he exclaimed, as the cross-reference came up with a name. "Dion Banks, age 24," he read, skimming Banks' extensive record.

Everything checked out. Everything except the last word in the file: deceased.

Franklin scowled. He quickly found the answer, and it made him grab the phone and dial frantically. The file told him *that Banks had been killed on the same date as the case. The information confirmed his theory.*

"Yeah, Detective Murray? Yeah, this is Detective Franklin. Listen, did you work a homicide involving one Dion Banks about a week ago? Okay, well, if you could, email me the report. I think it may have some connection to the massacre of that family on Hurman. Thanks."

Franklin hung up, one step closer to solving the riddle.

Men in black with automatic weapons locked and loaded stealthily made their way toward their target, the beam of their infrared crisscrossing the grounds of the estate. She rode Vee with total abandonment, urging him deeper, her cries of passion filling the room. The Isley Brothers crooned in surround sound, but despite it all, Vee still heard. His eyes popped open a second before the slaughter. All he saw outside the patio window was a hit squad sent to murder him.

"Fuck!" he gritted, rolling the girl over and onto the floor as bullets shattered the windows and blew up the water bed Vee had just been occupying. "You muhfuckas want a war with me?!" Vee barked, then laughed like their presence was a joke.

He reached under the bed and pulled out a fully automatic .50-cal assault weapon, a weapon so powerful that without leaving the cover of the bed, he fired through the bed base, the wall, and the flesh of several assassins, who howled as the bullets lifted their spirits out of their bodies.

"Don't holla now, muhfuckas!" Vee taunted.

He looked around for the girl, but she was gone. Had she been a part of it? No time to think, only react.

He glanced around the bed frame. Except for the dead bodies, the patio was empty. He heard footsteps. Many footsteps moving in the house. They had sent everything they had.

Vee stood up and left the bedroom. They were pouring in like roaches from all directions. Too many to count, too many to beat.

"Stupid-ass nigguhs, when will you learn?! You can't kill me! I'm the devil's son!!" Vee boasted and let the automatic beast in his hands roar.

Bodies fell, shots were returned. Vee was hit again and again. He looked up into the face of Ty. Ty smirked menacingly.

"Game over, nigguh," Ty hissed.

"You can't beat us all," Tito added from another direction.

Vee looked around and saw Tre with Tito.

"You too, nigguh?" Vee yelled at Tre.

Tre shrugged like, "Always go with the odds."

"You can't win, son."

The words cut through Vee worse than any bullet.

He whirled around and saw Guy.

Despite the pain, Vee's pride wouldn't let him succumb.

"Fuck all y'all!" he spat, unloading his weapon in all directions.

They all fired back, simultaneously, riddling Vee's body, but still he stood open-armed, welcoming their assault.

"The devil's son! Nothin' can kill me!"

"Nothing except love," Cat said.

Vee spun around and came face to face with Cat, her gun aimed at his face.

"Cat?!" Vee gasped.

Then she pulled the trigger.

Vee woke up in a cold sweat, his heart beating in his ears. What did it all mean? It took him several moments before he realized his phone was ringing. He ignored it, covering his face with his hands trying to get his composure. It rang again.

Ty ... Tito ... Tre ... Cat ... even Guy? He knew from experience that his dreams had meaning. This dream was different. He had never been shot before in his dreams. The bullets always missed, disappeared, or simply couldn't touch him. This time they had.

What did it mean?

The phone rang again.

Out of aggravation, he snatched it off the nightstand and barked, "What?"

"Vee, it's me, Karrin. Are you okay?!"

Vee took a deep breath and lowered his tone.

"Yeah, I'm good. Just—what up?"

She could hardly contain her excitement.

"I've got good news! Are you ready?! I've found Cat!" Vee was speechless, not because of what she said, but the chill her words produced in him.

What did it mean?

CHAPTER 39

He got his first Mink before he could walk, and when he did walk, his first steps were in a pair of baby walking shoes made of ostrich.

"You gonna spoil that child rotten," was the comment Theresa often heard. To which she always replied, "This Eddie Bell's son; it's his goddamn birthright!"

Theresa dealt with Eddie's death by celebrating his being and not mourning his loss. Tito became her mode of expression, the canvas on which she proceeded to paint the portrait of Eddie. In her mind, Tito would be Eddie Bell II, and he proved his potential at nine years old.

Devotion/someone by your side
Devotion/when things aren't going right
Devotion/someone to be your friend
Devotion/girl, through thick and through thin

The jukebox pumped the hit by Tin City through the

crowded bar, the hottest bar in the 80s for Harlem's elite. Theresa was there holding a convo with some of her girlfriends, all of them looking deliciously expensive. Theresa had not only been married to the game, she had a game of her own. Backed by Tito Sarducci, she ran numbers and a lucrative cocaine side business. Her money was long and she lavished it on Tito and her young twins, Brooklyn and Asia.

The place was packed this particular Saturday. Theresa showed off young Tito. She had him decked out in a royal-blue silk suit, a pair of black gator loafers, and a black Kangol cap that she hated but he loved.

"Theresa, you know you ain't 'posed to have that boy in no bar," the bartender reprimanded her, worrying more about his liquor license more so than the morality of motherhood.

"Nigguh, one day my baby gonna own this bar!" she and her entourage laughed.

Someone played Cameo's "Candy," and it made Theresa howl like she was in pain.

"Oooh, that's my song! Come on, baby, dance wit' your Mama," she said to Tito, taking his hand but never getting off the stool.

"Ma, I don't like to dance," Tito replied, like he was too cool to boogie.

"I'll dance wit' you," she heard someone say.

She looked up as the dude approached. Theresa knew him instantly.

Claude Jenkins. He was from the Polo Grounds. He had a promising basketball career ahead of him back in the day and his name rang bells at the Rucker. But he went up North on a bank robbery conviction. He was just coming home.

"I can see it when you walk, it takes over me," he sang off key. His words slurred by his drunkenness. "Come on sweet thang," he belted.

He tried to take her hand, but she pulled away.

"Nigguh, you ain't gotta touch me to speak," Theresa snapped.

He twisted up his face like her words hurt.

"Mrs. Bell, Mrs. Bell, don't be so mean. What's a man gotta do to have a moment of your time as a down payment on the rest of your evening?"

Theresa looked him up and down. He was still wearing the style of clothes popular before he went to prison. She laughed in his face.

"Nigguh, you gots to be jokin'," she replied dismissively and turned away.

Her girls laughed. Claude stiffened to the embarrassment, but hisdrunkenness made him bold. He leaned in close to Theresa and crooned, "Baby, baby, don't you know/It's a cold world out there/All I'm trying to do is be your coat/Can I be what wraps you up and protects you from the cold?"

Theresa nodded her head and glared at him.

"Claude, if you don't get the hell away from me wit' that lame-ass shit!"

Claude stood up straight, wobbled, then adjusted his belt.

"Bitch, you better check yo' goddamn self! The God is home, you understand, and nobody can protect you from God, not even the Eye-Talians. I don't give a fuck about them, 'cause, bitch, you been chose!" Claude ranted, then took her forcefully by the arm.

Theresa threw her drink in his face without hesitation, and Claude retaliated with a vicious backhand, drawing blood and knocking Theresa off her stool. Her girlfriends began to react, but Claude pulled out a .38 and backed them off. Theresa tried to grab her clutch, but Claude snatched her by the throat.

"See, bitch?! Nothing can protect you from God!" he hissed. "See what you made me do!?"

"Nig—," she gasped, clawing at his grip, "you betta kill—"

"Or what, huh? Or what?" he taunted.

All of her girls carried razors, but only she carried a gun. She kept it in her clutch. A pink two-shot Derringer .32. Tito knew she carried it. He knew how to use it because she had shown him, he wasn't scared. He subtly reached for her purse and took out the gun, never taking his eyes off Claude. He aimed and put the cold steel to the back of Claude's skull.

"Get off my Mama," Tito gritted firmly, both little hands aiming the gun.

Claude glanced over his shoulder.

"You little motherfucka! If you don't—"

Boom! Boom!

Two shots. Point blank. Blood splattered across Theresa's face and Tito's suit. Everybody in the bar was shocked except Theresa. Tito was Eddie Bell's son. She hugged him.

"Baby, are you okay?" she asked.

He nodded, looking at Claude's body twitch. His

only regret was that he couldn't kill the bastard again. Her girls helped her up.

"Ain't none of you motherfuckas seen shit, you hear me? Not a goddamn thing! Let me find out otherwise and it'll be the last goddamn thing you see, trust me!" Theresa warned, then took Tito by the hand and led him out.

Since then, the story has been told many times, too many ways, but one thing is for sure: The legend of Tito Bell began with two shots at point-blank range.

"Thanks, baby," Tito said as his Nigerian Imani handed him and Ty their drinks.

"Anything else?" she inquired politely.

"Naw, baby, I'm good," Tito replied as he loosened his tie and took a sip of his drink. But as she started to walk away, he added, "Oh, yeah, see if you can get Vanya on the phone. Let her know I'm in Atlanta if she wants to meet."

She nodded, then left the room.

Tito and Ty were in Tito's high-rise penthouse at the East Point in Atlanta's posh Bankhead section. He had just bought the spot in order to oversee his planned expansion into the Southeast, courtesy of the Simmons family. Besides, he needed to get out of New York for a while since the Sarducci slaughter was the topic of every newspaper journalist and TV reporter in the city. The other mob families were suffering the heat. The media called it the beginning of a mob war. They didn't know it was really the end of one.

"Damn, cuz, I gotta get me one of those," Ty chuckled, referring to the Nigerian goddess. "What is she? The maid? The assistant?"

"Fam, she whateva I need her to be when I need it," Tito winked, settling into the plush leather armchair and resting his drink on the arm.

They both laughed.

"Oh, shit, in that case I got plenty of those," Ty cracked.

Tito sipped his drink.

"Now that New York is behind us, you gonna tell me what it is with you and that dude Jay?"

Ty knew this conversation was coming soon, so he was prepared to use it to his advantage.

Ty downed his drink the replied, "His name ain't Jay, it's Vee."

"Okay," Tito said like, *And?*

"He used to work for me before I did my bid," Ty answered vaguely.

"So what, you fell out over money? Nigguh crossed you or somethin'?"

"Naw," Ty replied, getting up to refresh his drink, "we fell out over Kev."

Ty was purposely drawing it out because he wanted that element of drama to play out in Tito's emotional reaction. He was definitely his mother's son.

"Fam, I don't get it," Tito said, impatience subtly coloring his tone. "Why would Kev—"

"He killed him."

"Huh? Kev killed who?"

"Naw, cuz, I'm talkin' about Vee, yo. Vee killed Kev." Ty dropped the bomb.

Tito stood up. "What? How the …" Tito was thrown for a total loop, just like Ty knew he would be. "Then what the fuck was he doin' wit' Guy?! What the fuck is he doin' still breathing?"

Ty shrugged like, "Ask Guy. He stopped me from killin' the nigguh—twice."

"What the fuck is Unk thinkin?"

"He don't want us to kill his son," Ty grimaced. "Vee is Guy's son."

Now Tito's head was really spinning, but at least things were beginning to piece together. He thought back to the conversation with Gloria.

I just told you Guy let him go, let him walk away.

"His son?" Tito echoed incredulously. "The faggot that killed Kev was his own brother? Your brother?"

"Yeah," Ty replied simply, lying and telling the truth at the same time. He wasn't ready to tell Tito about his own paternity.

"Wow."

Ty poured Tito a drink—in more ways than one. He handed him the glass.

"I'm tellin' you, cuz, Pops ain't thinkin' clear. This nigguh killed Kev! But yet and still he on some long-lost shit?" Ty shook his head, then looked Tito in the eyes. "Ain't no tellin' how Pops gonna carry this nigguh, yo. But I know what needs to happen."

Tito nodded and sipped his drink. He understood instantly.

"But how would Guy take it?"

"How else can he take it? Once it's done, it's done, feel me? Fuck he gonna do, bring the nigguh back from the dead?" Ty cracked without a smile.

"Okay, so let's make it happen," Tito shrugged.

"Then you need to holla at your man Tre," Ty suggested, exactly what he had in mind the whole time.

Tito drank his drink, contemplating Ty's words. Tre was his man, but Vee was Tre's man. Your man's man ain't your man, he quipped to himself. He wondered how Tre would react if it was a go. Tito stood to benefit in two ways. He would help Ty solidify his place with Guy and, therefore, this deal with Tito. And on the back end, since he was about to talk to Tre about a piece of his porn game, removing Vee meant more money on that end as well.

The Nigerian goddess entered the room.

"Vanya said she looks forward to it. She suggested the lounge at 9."

"Cool. And, Anya, get Tre on the line ASAP."

Ty downed his drink to conceal his smile.

●●●●●●

Every ring vibrated her heart.

How long could she hold out? Every time the phone rang, Ty's picture appeared. That smile, those eyes, those sexy-ass lips. The way he would use them to …

The distance was torture for Karrin, but ignoring him was unbearable. She had not answered the last four times he called, but this time she just couldn't do it again.

"Hello, Ty," she answered, nervously biting her bottom lip.

"Baby, what's up?" Ty said. He felt relieved to finally hear her voice but at the same time, angry because he knew now she had been ignoring him.

But he knew he couldn't pass on her. He had to smother her with love, kill her with kindness, just in case he had to kill her for real.

"I'm … I'm ok. Ty, I'm sorry I haven't been answering your calls. I was just scared," Karrin admitted.

"Of me?" Ty chuckled lightly.

Should I be? her mind said, but she answered, "No, no, just … I didn't know what to do."

"Ma, don't worry. Everything is good, yo."

"But … Debra."

Hearing the name made Ty cringe. He missed his mother terribly.

"I know, ma. But it's okay. I know who was behind it."

"Was it—?"

"Naw, baby, I told you, it's good. Where are you?"

Those three words represented the biggest one of Karrin's life. She loved Ty with all of her heart, but she was also a survivor. What if Ty was lying? What if, now that Debra was gone, Ty was sacrificing her to get in good with Guy and solidify his position? Hadn't he turned his back on her in prison? And what about Vee? If Vee found out she had told Ty where she was, there would be consequences.

"Baby?" Ty said after Karrin had hesitated for so long.

"I'm … I'm … I'm okay, baby," she demurred.

"But where are you?" he repeated.

A tear of fear mixed with regret fell from her eye.

"I … I can't tell you."

Inside, Ty boiled, but he tried to restrain it.

"Karrin, baby, this Ty. Why can't you tell me?"

The tears followed each other in quick succession.

"I love you, Ty. I have to go."

"Karrin."

"I ... I love you. I'm sorry," she sobbed.

Click.

"Karrin!" Ty screamed into the phone.

When he realized she was gone, he hurled his phone against the passenger's window as he drove, not caring if he smashed it or the window.

She was hiding from him. That was bad. She knew the truth. She could expose Debra and therefore him. He had to find her. She was a loose end he could no longer afford.

Vee pulled up to Guy's estate and parked the rental. He remembered the last time he was here, how heavily guarded the place was. He could see security was still tight but much more subtly situated. Many cars lined the U-shaped driveway and grassy front area for Guy's birthday picnic. He could hear music, children's laughter, and the smell of barbeque chicken and ribs.

Vee wouldn't have come if his mother hadn't called him, but in all honesty, he needed it. He needed a break from the madness because deep inside, he could feel a storm on the horizon. He already knew Durham was on fire. Several people had told him so, which is why he was in a rental. He had sold the Bentley; he got rid of every conceivable connection to Durham and the Wolf Pack. He was living from hotel to hotel. He felt like a fugitive. He didn't regret what he did to the Banks family. Treacherymust be dealt with severely, so come what may; he would deal with the consequences. Even though he wasn't worried about the investigation, he was on the run…and in a way, on the run from itself.

Vee approached the front door and was stopped by a giant of a man at the front door.

"Name," the dude stated firmly, less like a question and more like a command.

"Vee."

"Vee?"

"Vee."

The dude eyed him, then got on the radio.

Chirp. Chirp.

"Guy expectin' a Vee?"

Chirp Chirp.

"Let him in."

Chirp Chirp.

"Okay, Vee," the giant smirked.

Vee walked through the foyer, through a throng of bad-ass kids, and tipsy women to the back patio, just in time to hear:

Happy birthday, dear –

Where everybody else said "Guy," Shantelle yelled, "old man."

The crowd broke out into laughter while trying to finish the song. They were off beat, off key, slurred, and garbled, but they finished the song with nothing but love. When Guy bent down to blow out the candles, Shantelle blew them out with him. When they finished, Guy took her in his arms and kissed her, making her glow.

It was clear to Vee his mother was in love. Although

in a physical sense, she may have been a stranger, on a deeper meaningful level, he knew her like he knew himself. Seeing the two of them together answered a lot of unspoken questions.

Here were the two people who had given birth to him. His life was based on what they shared. Just as some are born to passionate one-night stands or a married couple, what he was born of was timeless. Even after twenty years, it was still strong. Vee felt like Shantelle deserved to be happy. At some point we all do, and when that opportunity comes, you grab it. He was the only thing standing in the way of the happiness.

My mother is in love with an informant.

My father is an informant.

The treachery for which he murdered the Banks family was no worse than the treachery of Guy's betrayal of the game. Vee literally flinched when he felt a powerful hand grab his shoulder jolting him out of his thoughts.

"Whoa, nephew," Hawk Bill chuckled. I might be old, but this goddamn left will sit you on yo' ass," he concluded, waving his fist playfully.

Vee saw he had balled up his fist on instance. He laughed and shook Hawk Bill's hand.

"What's up, Unk?"

"Relax, nephew, you wit' family now," Hawk Bill assured him.

"Goddammit, Guy, are you gonna let me tell the story, or are you gonna tell it?" Shantelle said playfully. Vee and Hawk Bill both looked at the couple.

"Yeah, you can say what you will about that nigguh,

and believe me, I done said plenty," Hawk Bill laughed, "but he love yo' momma, and sometimes that's all that really matters."

Vee looked at Hawk Bill, but Hawk Bill didn't notice that his words seemed to speak to Vee's dilemma, making Vee wonder if it was that obvious.

"There go my baby!" Shantelle exclaimed when she saw Vee. She rushed over and threw her arms around his neck and covered his face with Hennessey-flavored kisses.

"Come on, Ma," Vee resisted, happy to be with her but done with the overkill.

"Come on, Ma," she mockingly repeated. "Used to be the same way when you was little, wipin' my kisses off wit' your mannish ass."

Vee chuckled. Guy walked up.

"Vee. How you doin?" Guy greeted. He wanted to extend his hand, but the steel in Vee's gaze stopped him.

"What's up," Vee replied.

Shantelle felt the chill, but she knew they had to find their own way as men. She took Vee's arm.

"Come on, let me introduce you 'round," she said, walking Vee off.

Guy watched them walk away.

"Guy," Hawk Bill began.

"Yeah?"

"Tell me somthin'."

"Hmm?" Guy said, not taking his eyes off Vee.

"You think you made a mistake?" Hawk Bill asked. Guy knew he was referring to letting Vee live.

Guy gave Hawk Bill a curious look, paused, then turned back in Vee's direction. He never answered the question.

CHAPTER 40

Pimlico Racetrack in Baltimore County was one of Tre's favorite spots. He loved to bet on the horses. It was a habit he acquired in New York, an addiction sustained by O.T.B (off track betting).

"Tre, what does ' two dash one mean?" Fiyah questioned.

She, Tre and his clan of goons and porn queens came through Pimlico, ghetto classy. It was a warm night, and they all were looking good and turning heads.

Tre took the cigar out of his mouth.

"Those are the odds. The longer the odds, the more money you make if the horse wins," he explained.

"Oh. So why not just bet on those horses instead of two dash one or three dash one," she wanted to know.

Tre chuckled.

"Because the longer the odds, the less likely the horse is to win, baby. Don't get me wrong, a long shot pays off from time to time, but as a rule, put your money on the real thoroughbreds," he winked and slapped her juicy ass.

"I like Lady's Day," Fiyah surmised, surveying the names of the horses.

"It's Sleep's birthday, so believe me, it's gonna be lucky!" Tre exclaimed.

He had his goons placing the bets. Lady's Day lost. Tre looked up at the sky. "Sleep?" What the fuck are you doin?! She new to this, yo. Give her a break!"

The next three horses Fiyah bet on won, placed, or showed, including a 25-1 long shot that won her $7,500.

"I'm startin' to like this shit," Fiyah giggled, counting the wad of money in her hand.

"I'm sure you are, but you can't keep it," Tre told her.

"Can't keep it?"

Tre slid the money out of her grip.

"I told you it's Sleep birthday, yo. This for him.

Before she could ask, he answered by taking her winnings and his winnings, over $35,000 and tossing them into the crowd, causing a frenzy.

His entourage laughed and applauded the stunt.

"Courtesy of Sleep! Rest in peace, homey!" Tre barked, throwing a fist to the sky.

On their way out, Tre ran into Angelo. Angelo was a young pimp with a nice little stable. He had several of his chicks with him.

"What's up, my nigguh," Angelo greeted Tre.

Tre liked the young boy because his game was tight and he reminded him of himself at that age. Tre gave him a pound and a gangsta hug.

"What's up, yo? I see you, nigguh," Tre winked.

"Shit, nigguh, I see you too," Angelo replied, eyeing Fiyah up and down. "Ma, I'd trade ALL my aces for one queen."

Fiyah laughed.

"I'm sure you would."

"Hm-mmm," Angelo replied, licking his lips, then turning back to Tre. "Check this, my nigguh: Only the hand of God brought us together because what I propose is a match made in heaven. When can we rap a taste about this porn game, player?"

"Wheneva you ready."

"I'm ready now."

"Say no more. Bring your best by the studio and we can put something together."

"I like how you do business, my nigguh," Angelo replied, giving Tre a gangster hug. "Check for me tomorrow."

"That's what it is."

Angelo and his stable and Tre and his team parted in opposite directions. Had Tre paid closer attention to the cinnamon-brown chick in the black spandex dress, he would've recognized her as the female Vee said was his baby's mother, Cat.

"What?!"

"Tito, what the fuck?!"

Both responses were uttered simultaneously and in total disbelief. The twins couldn't believe their ears.

Tito had contemplated telling the twins ever since Gloria told him about Guy's betrayal. A part of him wanted to protect them. They were his baby sisters and he didn't want them subjected to a cold reality that they couldn't change or he couldn't change.

For them, on the other hand, he knew they deserved to know the truth. The twins hadn't been born when Eddie died. Theresa was seven months pregnant at the time. Still, Eddie was their father too. Besides, he respected them and knew neither would fold under the pressure of what was to come.

"But Tito … Uncle Guy???" Ann pleaded, trying to somehow make sense of this evil that men do.

Brooklyn wasn't having the same problem.

"Uncle?! That nigga ain't shit to us. We just ain't know it," she gritted, pacing the floor. Her anger was like a bubbling volcano. Its own movement caused it to explode.

"True indeed, yo. But I'm just sayin'," Asia shook her head. "This shit is crazy."

"What's crazy about it? The nigguh just killed the brother of the bitch he was fucking. Still, it wasn't his family," Brooklyn surmised. "And what about this bitch? That's who should go first, fuckin' her!" Brooklyn spat, not even willing to say Gloria's name."

Tito let them vent.

"And why you wait so long to tell us, Tito?" Asia asked. "Why the fuck you had us blind to his snake-ass shit?"

Tito looked at Asia.

"You trust me?" he shot back.

"Of course."

"That's why," he retorted brusquely. "Plus, I ain't want you flyin' off the handle and jumpin' the gun."

"What you mean, jumping the gun?" Brooklyn questioned, sensing an angle she didn't like. "Ain't no gun to jump! This getting handled from the jump."

"No."

"No?!"

"No," Tito repeated calmly.

"Tito, I swear to—"

"Look!" he barked, standing to his feet and glaring at Brooklyn and Asia alternately as he spoke. "He will die. This is without question but—"

"Everything after 'but' is bullshit," Brooklyn fumed.

Tito pointed at her and gave her a look. Brooklyn fell back.

"But," he emphasized, looking at Brooklyn, "we will complete this deal and we will take everything. He owes us that much."

"He gave us blood, Tito," Asia said. Although she wasn't as hotheaded as Brooklyn, she was surely more cold-blooded. Asia killed without emotion, Brooklyn killed because of it.

Tito nodded.

"I agree, but why stop there?"

"What about … her?" Brooklyn wanted to know.

"And Ty?" Asia nodded.

"Ty is his father's son," Tito replied, and they both understood the weight of his words. "As for Aunt Gloria, I leave that to y'all after it's all said and done."

"Then it is said and done," Brooklyn hissed, and they both understood the weight of her words.

"Mommy ain't to know about this, not now, maybe not ever," Tito instructed them, and they both accepted it without question. Before Brooklyn and Asia walked out, Tito said, "Brooklyn, don't worry. This will be handled."

"Then I'ma be the one to handle it when the time comes," she vowed.

Don't you remember you told me you loved me, baby
You said you'd be comin' back this way again, baby

Luther Vandross' "Superstar" played as Guy and Shantelle swayed softly to the classic.

"Guy."

He knew her so well that he knew what she was about to say from her tone alone.

"I tried, Shantelle. You see how he acted like he don't wanna talk."

Shantelle leaned back so she could look at him while they danced.

"Guy, he's young and full of blood, as the old folks say. You know how you nigguhs are. When they act like they don't care is when they care the most."

Guy pondered the jewel she dropped, begrudgingly.

"Yeah, I hear you," he grumbled.

Shantelle put her finger under Guy's chin softly and stopped dancing. "Baby, we a family full of strangers. Somehow, someway somebody gotta make the induction."

Vee made the rounds with Hawk Bill, meeting various members of his family on both sides, including his grandfather, Willie Simmons.

Willie had been eyeing Vee since he had arrived, sitting in his wheelchair smoking his ever-present cigar.

He watched Vee intently. He had killed Kev. Willie was there when Vee stood before them to answer for that. He didn't flinch.

Willie had looked into his eyes when Vee said, "You think it didn't fuck me up to know the same nigguh that wanted me dead was my own brother?"

Willie had seen it then, a defiant type of remorse ready to meet any consequences head on, yet at the same time wishing desperately that the action of cause had never happened. It made Willie think about generations full of actions and consequences, and in a way, seeing himself as the ultimate cause, and Kev's death as his ultimate consequence. That thought alone was what gave him the power to extend his hand to Vee and ask gruffly, "What's your name, boy?"

"Vee."

"Vee??? I ain't ask how you spell it, nigguh. I said what's your name," Willie growled in the tone only an old man could get away with.

Hawk Bill laughed. Vee chuckled lightly in spite of himself.

"Victor Murphy."

"Murphy? You some kin to Darryl Murphy, Tina Murphy and them?"

No, sir, I was raised by Miss Sadie Murphy, and she gave me her last name. She from — "

Willie cut him off.

"I know who Miss Sadie is," he replied, puffing out cigar smoke and thinking to himself, I also know what she do.

Willie looked Vee over. He knew Simmons blood.

He was Simmons blood, so he could tell Vee was full of Simmons blood.

"You ET yet?" Willie asked.

"ET?" Vee echoed.

"That's what I said. Is you ET yet?"

Vee looked at Hawk Bill, confused.

"Have I ET?"

"ET, nigguh. ET! Goddamn, is you deaf?! Is you ET?"

Hawk Bill broke with laughter seeing the confused, frustrated look on Vee's face.

"He askin' have you ate yet," Hawk Bill clarified.

Vee smirked.

"Naw, yo, I guess not."

"Well, go on get you something to ET" Willie instructed.

When Vee and Hawk Bill started to walk away, Willie said, "You killed my grandbaby."

Vee stopped. He looked Willie in the eyes, not with a challenge, but as a man. "What would you have done?"

"Hmm," Willie snorted. He puffed his cigar and rolled away.

"You handled that well, nephew," Hawk Bill intoned.

"Yeah," Vee mumbled.

The question reminded him of the wall between him and the Simmonses, and it made him mad at himself to think his coming would somehow surmount it.

"Willie understood, trust me. It's just gonna take time. But listen, let me ask you somethin'. You ever heard of the Hardy family or Young Hardy?" Hawk Bill inquired.

"Who?"

Hawk Bill nodded knowingly.

"Yeah, I figured that."

"Figured what?"

Hawk Bill explained what happened to Ty's mother and how Hardy had come through bragging about doing it. He told Vee that Hardy claimed Ty killed his whole family.

"And that's when you came up. He said Kev thought maybe you and your people was usin' Hardy to get at Guy," Hawk Bill concluded.

Mentioning Kev's name in that context made Vee think of Banks. Banks was Kev's mole, therefore Kev had no reason to not know exactly who and what the Wolf Pack was doing. Vee recognized instantly what Ty was trying to do. Ty had something to do with the attempt on Guy's life because Karrin had told him. He saw no reason to tell Guy, or even Hawk Bill, because to him it was a Simmons family problem. And although he may've been a Simmons by blood, he wasn't family, so it wasn't his problem. With Guy being an informant and Ty trying to kill his own father, Vee shrugged it off, figuring they deserved each other.

His only concern was his mother.

"Unk, make sure Shantelle is okay. Keep an eye on her," Vee told Hawk Bill.

"That goes without saying, but what's up?" Hawk Bill asked, sensing more than just a general concern.

Vee shrugged.

"Like Miss Sadie used to say, every closed eye ain't sleep and every open eye ain't seein', you know?"

Vee was telling Hawk Bill, without telling him, the

answer was right in front of his face. Hawk Bill understood, although he didn't fully grasp the meaning. Hawk Bill's own sense of loyalty wouldn't let him see how conniving your own blood can be.

"Oh, and, Unk," Vee said, "how can I get at this nigguh Hardy? I'm the enemy, remember? Wolf Pack. Maybe he believes that bullshit in the '48 Laws of Power' and thinks the enemy of my enemy is my friend."

Hawk Bill smiled. He thought Vee wanted to use the Wolf Pack façade to get back at Hardy, but Vee only wanted to use it to get at Hardy. He had his own use for him.

"I'm on it, nephew."

Meanwhile, Young Hardy was using his mind. Day by day, murder for murder, he was getting closer to the edge. He lived by the gun. He was obsessed with one thought: killing Ty. Every day he replayed the event that led up to his family's death. He could see in hindsight exactly where Ty's tone changed and how even then Hardy had sensed it.

"Why I ain't yank on this nigguh??" Hardy had cursed himself for not pulling his gun when he felt the vibe.

But he knew the answer. His love and trust for Kev made him slip. He looked up to Kev, idolized him. He would've died for Kev. But in the end, what did it matter? Kev didn't hesitate to flip on Hardy. The pain of that alone was enough to kill love for any nigguhs in Hardy's heart. But killing his family made him a merciless animal that lived for only one thing: revenge.

"Daddy, why we can't have pizza?" the pretty little four-year-old pouted as her father picked her up.

The young baller, his daughter, and baby mother were entering their condo in Durham. The baller worked for Ty. He was one of his block lieutenants in Durham. He was feared and respected. It was broad daylight. All of these factors gave him a sense of safety that real predators prey upon.

As he opened the door, he was dazed by the butt of a pistol. His baby mama started to scream but a gloved hand covered her mouth and a forearm chocked her. Four men in black bandanas over their mouths shoved the family inside.

"Yo! What the fuck?" the baller protested, taken totally by surprise.

He felt a hand snatch his gun off his waist.

"Please," the female sobbed, "my baby ain't got nothin' to do with this!"

"You're right," Hardy hissed from behind his mask.

Boom!

The point-blank head shot blew the child's innocent brains all over the mother's face. The taste of her own child's blood made her pass out and hit the floor with a thud.

"Ohhhh, myyy Godddd!" the dude moaned like a mortally wounded animal.

Hardy kicked him in the face.

"Shut the fuck up!" he hissed, glad to see his own pain of losing a child reflected in someone else's eyes. "Now do you think I'm playin?!"

The dude sobbed and didn't answer. Hardy put his gun to his head. "Do you?"

The dude was in shock. He didn't answer because he couldn't, not because he was being tough. Hardy misunderstood.

"Oh, you still think it's a game?!" Hardy smirked menacingly, happy for a chance to inflict more pain.

Hardy snatched up the baby mama and smacked her awake. Her eyes opened but she wasn't seeing, she wasn't feeling, she wasn't there. Hardy bent her over the arm of the couch, snatched her pants off, spread her legs and rammed his dick in her pussy.

"Yeah, nigguh! You see?! You see?! This ain't a game!"

The only person who understood the connection between the rape and the reason they were there was Hardy. He wanted to inflict pain, pure and simple. He had to release a little every day just so he wouldn't blow his own brains out.

"Now tell me! Where the fuck is Ty?!" he demanded. The dude looked at him pleadingly.

"I swear man, I-I don't know."

"You don't?"

Boom!

One shot in the back of her head snuffed out whatever life was left in her and coated the couch with her blood. On the other end, her body spasmed and her bowels released and leaked on Hardy.

Hardy backed away in disgust, looking at the shit on his shirt and stomach. "Bitch!" he cursed the lifeless body, then emptied the clip in her corpse.

Hardy used his shirt to wipe off the shit, took it off and threw it in dude's face.

"Where is he???" Hardy repeated.

"I don't know."

Hardy turned away and headed for the back of the house.

"Kill that piece of shit!"

Boom! Boom!

Two shots ended the slaughter. The four of them ransacked the house, taking jewelry, money, and a couple bundles of heroin and mid-sized safes.

On the way out, Hardy grabbed the dude's phone, hoping Ty's number was in it.

⬤⬤⬤⬤⬤⬤

"I know, right? I knew we would find her. Yeah, I'm sure he will call back. When are you comin' back? okay. no, no, I'm good, I was just … okay, see you then."

Click.

Karrin hung up from speaking to Vee. When she turned around, Jatiah was smiling at her.

"What?" Karrin asked.

"Nothin'," Jatiah smirked.

"What?" Karrin repeated.

"You feelin' him, ain't you?"

"Who?" She tried to play stupid.

"Oh, now you a owl. Vee, that's who," Jatiah snickered.

"No," Karrin replied, like the thought never crossed her mind.

"Vee like a brother to me."

"Hmm-mm," Jatiah said. "I had a lot of brothers like that. Notice the word 'had.'"

Karrin laughed, catching her meaning.

"No, for real for real, he gotta baby by my cousin, Cat. I mean," she added sadly, "they had a baby."

Karrin explained about Vee and Cat and how Cat had lost the baby, then disappeared from the hospital, and how the guy had called and hopefully they had found her.

"Wow. That must've been hard on the brother," Jatiah commented.

"It was."

"I hope y'all find her. But on the real, Vee is a cutie," Jatiah winked.

Karrin smiled but didn't answer. She didn't need to. It was written all over her face.

CHAPTER 41

Six months earlier. A week and a day after the Banks family was murdered.

Franklin had gotten three for the price of one. Three unsolved murders instead of just one. It was the kind of bargain no one optioned for.

Detective Murray had explained to him that when they received the call about Banks' body in the car in the parking lot of a complex in Raleigh, they received a second call about a young couple found dead in an apartment in the same complex. All three had been killed with the same weapon, and the same way. Head shots, execution style.

In the car there had been no signs of struggle. In the apartment, no kind of forced entry. The only clue was a strange one.

"And get this," Detective Murray told him, "we found several hairs in the trunk of the car."

"Hairs?" Franklin echoed.

Murray nodded.

"African American, presumably female."

Franklin sat in his car at the apartment complex. He was parked in the same space Banks had parked in. The sun was going down and he was listening to John Coltrane's *A Love Supreme* album. It always helped him think.

"Why were you here?" he asked himself aloud, trying to put himself in Banks' position, minus the head shot.

"It wasn't random. The white couple's death in the apartment confirmed that. How were they involved? How did the killer, or killers, get in? And who the hell was in the trunk?"

Franklin had more questions than answers. The most intriguing being, who was in the trunk? At first he thought it was the owner of the car. The car had been stolen from Goldsboro, but it belonged to a middle-aged Mexican male.

Then he thought it was someone Banks may have killed and dumped along with whomever killed him.

Franklin was giving validity to that theory until he saw the apartment manager approach the apartment directly across from the apartment F and affix something to the door. He got out and quickly crossed the parking lot.

"Excuse me. Excuse me, Mr. Jones," Franklin called out.

Mr. Jones, a middle-aged black man, stopped and turned to him.

"Hi. Remember me? Detective Franklin. We talked last night."

"Yeah, I remember. What can I do for you?"

"Just curious — what were you posting on that door?"

Mr. Jones shrugged.

"Eviction notice. Why?"

Franklin's mind processed the information quickly.

"And ... are you familiar with the occupant or occupants of that residence?"

"I'm familiar with every tenant here, for the most part. It was a young black couple living here. I think they had a baby, but I ain't sure."

Franklin's ears perked up when he heard the words "young black couple."

"Mr. Jones, how long has it been since you've seen the couple?"

Mr. Jones looked off like he was contemplating the question.

"I don't know, a month or so. Seems so. The dude, I almost never saw him. Struck me as the thuggish type. But her? I'd say it's been about a month."

Franklin's adrenaline was racing like it always did when a case clicked in his head.

"Mr. Jones, is there any way I could maybe take a look in that apartment? I think it may have some connection to the murders a month ago."

"Well," Mr. Jones began, skeptically.

Franklin tried to convince him.

"Listen, you can come in with me, and I won't touch a thing. I promise, I just want to take a look around."

"Detective, I would sure love to help, but these courts nowadays, they so keen on property rights and such. Like the landlord don't have no rights. I remember – " Mr. Jones began, but Franklin cut him off.

"I understand, Mr. Jones. I'll just get a warrant."

"That's fine."

●●●●●●

Apartment G … young black couple … eviction. Could the hair in the trunk be hers? If so, why come back? Unless … did the couple in apartment F see too much? Victims of circumstance? Collateral damage?

These were the thoughts going through Franklin's mind as he drove. He had been a detective long enough to know to trust his instincts, and his instincts were telling him the answers were in apartment G.

He pulled up to what he called his oasis in the urban desert, A.M.E Baptist Church. Franklin was a strong believer in the gospel of Christ. His was a simple faith. He didn't flaunt it as proof of moral superiority, nor did he hide it from the modernity of cynicism. He just lived it to the best of his ability.

Franklin committed his Wednesday nights to teaching a class to the church youth. It was a class based on how to apply the gospels to being young and black. It wasn't that he had any special qualifications. He wasn't a biblical scholar. He was just the only black man in the congregation willing to do it.

"Brother Franklin, how are you this evening?" Reverend Moore greeted him warmly, with a smile and a firm handshake.

"I'm good, Reverend. How are you?"

"Fine, brother, just fine. The children are waiting on you in the back," the Reverend told him.

Franklin nodded.

"And Sister Jenkins has asked if you would speak to her son, Darnell. Seems like he's been having a lot of trouble in school."

"I will," Franklin assured him.

"And, Brother Franklin, I just want to say thank you. I know witnessing all the pain man can inflict tries every ounce of your faith," the Reverend surmised.

Franklin thought about what he said, then replied, "Actually, Reverend Moore, it confirms my faith." He then walked away.

There were usually seven kids, five boys and two girls. Their attendance was consistent because their mothers used the Wednesday night program as a free babysitter. The kids liked

Franklin and he loved them. They learned a lot. He learned more. He spoke about man gaining the whole world at the expense of his soul.

After the program, he held Darnell behind.

"What's going on, D?" Franklin greeted him.

The lanky twelve-year-old mumbled, "I'm good."

"What I tell you about talking with your head down? Look a man in the eye when you talk to him," Franklin reminded him.

Darnell jerked his head and met Franklin's glare.

"I said I'm good."

Franklin saw a look in Darnell's eyes he had never seen: rebellion. He was at that age in the ghetto that made you subject to grown-up decisions before you had a chance to grow up.

"That ain't what your mother says about school."

Darnell sucked his teeth but didn't answer. Franklin crouched down to his level and inquired, "What's up, D? I thought we were cool? You can't talk to me no more?"

"I'm just sayin'," Darnell mumbled, looking away from Franklin.

"Speak your mind, young brother," Franklin urged.

Darnell looked at Franklin and blurted, "You the police."

He said it like that was all the explanation needed. Franklin chuckled. "Okay, but I've been the police since you met me. I was the police when I took you to see LeBron play the Bobcats, right? And when I took you to King's Dominion. What's the problem now?"

Darnell huffed.

"It just is, man. Can I go?"

Franklin studied him momentarily, then he got it.

"Oh, okay, I see. You don't want your friends to think you talkin' to the police, huh?"

Darnell wouldn't look at him, but his body language said he was right.

"Because the police is the bad guy, huh? Always locking people up for just tryin' to eat, huh?" Franklin quipped.

"Why we need police anyway, yo? Any man should be able to handle his," Darnell boasted.

"I feel you. But what about a woman? A grandmother? Your grandma!" Darnell looked Franklin in the eyes.

"I can take care of mine, yo."

"Yeah? What about a grandma that doesn't have a grandson that can handle his?" Franklin probed.

Darnell shrugged. "Get a dog," he said.

"I see," Franklin replied, taking out his iPhone. "I got something here I want you to see."

Franklin pulled up the pictures of the Banks family, raw and uncut. He held the phone under Darnell's nose like smelling salts to an unconscious victim. When Darnell saw the picture of Banks' grandmother covered in blood, her eyes stabbed out, head hanging on by the tendon in her neck, he jumped back.

Yo, man!"

Franklin grabbed his arm.

"Naw, naw, look at it! Look!" He went through all four victims, jerking Darnell's attention back when he looked away.

"This is the other side of the game! Where no matter how you handle yours, nothing you do can bring them back!" Franklin barked.

Darnell snatched away, a look of disgust on his face. Franklin wasn't sure he had reached Darnell, but he knew he'd never forget those pictures.

Coordinating an investigation between two cities is hard, especially when those two cities were Durham and Raleigh. Getting the warrant threatened to take too much red tape, but Detective Murray helped out. It was his case, his jurisdiction, therefore he felt didn't need a warrant. Murray accompanied Franklin back to apartment G and got him in.

Franklin wasn't to be disappointed.

The first thing that struck him was that the place was definitely a baller's crib. The amenities, the plasma TVs, the plush leather décor, and high-priced clothes screamed illegal business. Even the baby's room had a plasma TV. He found out the lease was in the name of Evelyn Richards, yet the mail was all in the name of Kianna Richards.

"Probably an aunt or a crackhead with good credit," Franklin surmised wrongly.

But what made it all come together were the pictures. They sat on the coffee table still in the Eckerd's envelope, newly developed. Pictures of Bike Week and various guys that he would later learn were the Wolf Pack and Ty, minus Vee. Vee didn't take pictures, precisely for the reason now coming to fruition: identification.

Most dudes in the game don't realize the importance of avoiding cameras, all cameras. The next flick is a mug shot. Vee knew he was in none of the pictures.

"Recognize any of these guys?" Franklin asked Murray.

Murray took the flicks and shuffled through them.

"No ... no ... familiar ... now her I'd like to know,"

he chuckled, then his eyes got big for another reason. "Bingo! There's your Wolf Pack connect!"

He showed Franklin a picture of Ty with two chicks, one under each arm.

"That's Tyquan Simmons, the numero uno, el Jere of the Wolf Pack," Murray explained.

"Tyquan Simmons? I've heard J- Love or maybe some guy named Vee, but never a Tyquan. Interesting."

Then he saw it. In the master bedroom. Vee's only moment of weakness. A family portrait of him, Cat, and their just-born son, Taheem. Cat had a fit until Vee relented. That one smile would lead to his downfall.

But that wasn't all.

Franklin eyed the pictures hard. There was no mistaking. He was one hundred percent sure, and because of what he saw, it was personal.

Murray came in the bedroom, just closing his phone.

"Hey, Franklin, guess what just came up on that car we found Banks' body in."

⚫⚫⚫⚫⚫⚫

"Ohh, I love you, Lil' Eddie, I love you!" the girl gushed as Tito plowed her deep with his hard, young meat.

They were in the stairwell of her building, one landing before the roof. Isolated in a dilapidated building. Tito had his pants down around his ankles, and her tennis skirt up around her stomach, exposing her pretty brown round and the key to her heart. He had her facing the wall, ass poked out while he long stroked her emotions.

"I do, Lil' Eddie, I do! Oohh, tell me you love me!" she gasped, receiving only his grunts as a reply. "Eddie," she whined.

"Shut up, bitch," he growled, lost in the lust of his thrust.

"Yeah, baby just like that," Tito growled, fucking her harder until their slapping skin sounded like applause.

"It's yours, baby!"

"I know," Tito hissed, as his stomach knotted and the sensation of sweet release made his body spasm, filling the condom with his spent seed.

Tito pulled off the condom with his thumb and forefinger, then discarded it amongst the other condoms, crack vials, and headless matches. The girl slid on her panties and adjusted her skirt, then threw her arm around Tito's neck. She tried to kiss him but he turned his head.

"Why you frontin'? It's yours," she smirked.

"Yeah, but I don't want to suck it," he retorted.

She studied his features with admiration. His curly hair, his light brown eyes, his smooth mocha complexion. She bent to his neck like a vampire trying to suck his neck. Tito knew she was trying to put a hickey on him, so he untangled her arms from around him and backed away, fixing his pants.

"Yo, chill," he chuckled.

"Why? Ain't I'm your girl?"

"Naw, yo, I go wit' Tina. If she see a hickey, she gonna spaz on you," Tito replied, fighting back a smile.

The truth was Tina meant no more to him than the nameless girl in his face. He just liked to have girls fighting over him.

She sucked her teeth, shifted her weight, struck a stance, and put her hand on her hip.

"I wish that bitch would open her mouth. Just wait 'til I see her."

"Come on. Let's go."

As they reached street level, she asked, "So you gonna call me?"

"Call you what?"

"I mean call me on the phone, boy. Stop playin," she snickered.

"Sure, I'll call you. What's your name?" he asked, flaunting his smirk.

"Nigguh, you know my name!" she huffed indignantly.

He shrugged. "I forgot."

She turned away and walked off so he wouldn't see her embarrassed tears. Tito stepped off nonchalantly. He really didn't care at sixteen. He was arrogant for no reason other than being Eddie Bell's boy. They even called him Lil' Eddie. Theresa spoiled him rotten. When sheepskins came out, he had one in every color, with the hat to match. When Espree scooters came out, he was the first on 116th Street to have one.

His Gucci link dookie rope was 10K hollow from Canal Street. It was 14K solid from the Jews in Diamond District (where dookie ropes originated). He was young, fly, and the heir apparent to a Harlem legend. The older generation would say, "There go Eddie Bell's boy."

Tito's friends would say, "There go my nigguh Lil' Eddie."

And all the young girls (and quite a few older ones) would gush, "There goes my baby!"

116th between 7th and 8th over to Morningside was his small slice of heaven.

"Yo, Tito, what you know about this, money?" Tito's friend, Jerome bragged.

Jerome was with a group of neighborhood kids in front of Tito's building. Jerome was a young cat too, but he hustled. He was only seventeen, but he worked for a dude named Rich Porter who was already legend status in Harlem.

Jerome didn't really respect Tito because to him Tito was just living off his father's name. He was the only one who wouldn't call him Lil' Eddie. He had been born with a ghetto silver spoon, so Jerome always made it a point to flaunt his achievement in Tito's face.

Jerome had just bought his first Benz. It was a Mercedes Benz 190. It was the cheapest model Benz made, but still, it was a Benz. Jerome had just bought it, so it still had factory everything, but the glistening cocaine-white paint job held the potential of ghetto fab.

"Word, money, check this out. I'ma pipe this shit out, throw the Alpine goose neck in it, and the gold BBs!" Jerome bragged.

"You gonna tint the windows?" someone foolish asked.

Jerome looked at him like he had two heads.

"Tint the windows? Slap yourself. You don't tint windows on a white car. Besides, I want nigguhs to know who drivin'," Jerome replied, taunting Tito with a wink.

Tito was heated. He hated that Jerome got a car first. But he held his composure.

"Yo, you got that off, G," Tito congratulated him, heading up the stairs of his building.

He took the stairs two at a time, fueled by his hurt pride, unjust anger, and spoiled resentment. As soon as he came through the door, he blurted out, "Ma, I want a car."

Theresa was sitting on the couch counting money. She didn't respond.

"Ma," he repeated more firmly, "I know you hear me."

"I'm busy," she answered, never looking up.

He looked at the twins on the floor looking at each other. He knew what was coming next. A fight. You would think they hated each other as much as they fought for no reason, but they loved each other to death. They were just bad.

"Ma, you can't count later? I want a car," Tito gritted.

Theresa looked up, aggravated.

"Boy, didn't you hear me say I was busy? And you," she hissed, pointing at the twins, "do it again."

They stopped wrestling, got up, and went in the back so they could kill each other in peace.

"Now, what is it, boy?"

"A car. Jerome just got a Benz, Ma. I'm sayin', it ain't gotta be a Benz yet, but I'm almost seventeen. I need a car. How I look on a scooter?" he huffed.

Theresa chuckled and echoed the one word he said that said it all.

"Yet."

She eyed him inquisitively, with a smile and a look of disgust on her face. She didn't regret spoiling him. That was for her as much as it was for him. But she knew it was time for all that to change.

"Who are you?" she asked simply.

"What you talkin' about? I'm me," he answered, confused by her question.

"What does that mean?" Theresa pressed.

"I'm Eddie Bell's boy," he replied proudly, like he always did. "You used to be Eddie Bell's boy," Theresa told him coldly as she stood up.

Her words were like a slap in the face, but it would take him a while to realize they were meant as a wake-up call, not a diss.

Tito looked at her blankly.

"Ma, what's wrong?"

"You," she spat, lighting a Newport 100. "You."

She wasn't making sense to him. He charged it to P.M.S., but she wasn't bleeding.

"You buggin', yo," he said dismissively, then turned to walk away.

"Get out."

He heard the words but couldn't connect the gravity of their meaning to the calm of the moment. Tito turned back.

"Huh?"

"I said get out. Get out of my house wit' your hand out. Wit' your beggin', whinin', me-me-me bullshit, and let the fuck go of my apron," Theresa said firmly and calmly.

"Ma? Wh-what did I do??" Tito wanted to know.

"Nothin'," she barked, and that one word said it all.

Tito hung his head because he knew exactly what she meant.

"What I'm 'posed to do?"

Theresa went back to counting money. Tito glanced at her. He looked down the hall and saw the twins looking at him passively, sucking their thumbs, holding hands.

"Okay," he nodded.

Tito turned for the door. The twins ran and grabbed his legs and began crying.

"And take off my shit."

Tito eyed his mother. She inhaled the smoke.

"You want me to walk out naked?" he gritted.

"Asia get some of your uncle's clothes."

Asia ran off to comply. Theresa's brother had been in prison for three years, so his styles were three years old, plus he was three inches shorter than Tito.

Tito and Theresa held each other's gaze. He could see the determination and finality in her eyes, but he could also see the pain. She saw the hurt in his eyes, but she saw the burst of purpose forming in his eyes as well. In the mother-son world, they had reached inevitability.

Asia brought back the clothes. Tito took them, nodded at his mother, and put them on.

"Damn, money," Jerome laughed, "what the fuck happened to you?"

Tito stepped out of the building looking nothing like he looked when he went in. Gone were the Gucci link and three-finger rings, the Polo shirt and glasses, Calvin Klein and Jordans. Now he wore a tight-ass Members Only coat with some high-water Lees.

The other dudes wanted to laugh, but the look in Tito's eyes made them stifle it. Only Jerome went at him.

"Is it Halloween? Goddamn, money, what happened? I know this ain't Lil' Eddie," Jerome taunted.

It was the first time Jerome called him Lil' Eddie. It would also be the last.

Blah!

Tito caught Jerome in the mouth, snapping his head back, then followed with another blow. Jerome was dazed, but he was OK. The two of them began exchanging blows in the middle of the street, holding up traffic and drawing a crowd. No one broke them up. When it was over, and they were both bloody but unbowed, Tito caught his breath, and said, "My name Tito," and walked away.

Years later when they'd meet again as equals, they would laugh about it, but at the moment, no one cracked a smile.

Tito glanced up and saw his mother looking out the window.

He looked away and turned the corner.

As he walked, he thought about where he was going to go. He could go to either of his grandmothers' houses. Or he could go stay with this older chick he'd been fucking. He even thought of his uncle Guy down South. But he kept thinking about his mother saying he did nothing.

It was like a challenge, and if not heeded, a prophecy.

He would be damned if it would be a prophecy. Tito knew only one place he could go: the Bronx.

His man Tradero AKA Tre lived in the Bronx. They had met through mutual friends and clicked, although Tradero was two years older than Tito. Tradero ran a few weed gates in the Bronx and Upper Manhattan. A weed gate is an apartment used strictly for distribution. Like the drive-thru window of a fast-food joint. One person sat behind the reinforced steel door of an apartment. The customer slid the money under the door and received his purchase the same way. Tradero wasn't getting rich, but he was doing damn good.

Tito explained the situation to him. Tradero was ready to hold him down without blinking.

"Say no more, my nigguh, I got you," Tre assured him. "I got a spot on 190th that I could give – "

Tito cut him off.

"Naw, G, I got my own spot. 145th and Amsterdam," Tito smirked.

Tre looked at him. "My nigguh, the dreads got one-four-fifth sewed up. They makin' crazy money over there."

"Can you think of a better market to set up shop in?" Tito quipped.

Tre chuckled and shook his head.

"Go hard and go home, huh?"

"Naw, just go hard," Tito replied without smiling.

They shook on the beginning.

For the first few weeks things went smoothly. 145th and Amsterdam was known to be the weed spot, and the Jamaicans ran the block. The situation was tense, but no one moved on Tito and his young team until one dread named Smoke got fed up with their presence.

Tito was coming out of the building with two of his young gunners. They had just dropped off a few pounds at their gate because business was booming. Smoke crossed the street with that long Jamaican stride, swinging a machete, which the dreads call an outlast.

"Look ere, pussy boy, seen? Ya no stay here seen?! We run tings ere, yankee bwoh! Ya nah wan trouble wit' us, seen?!" Smoke bassed, gesturing wildly with the machete.

Tito listened without saying a word. Smoke wanted to intimidate the young boys. He should've just walked up and started swinging his blade.

"I don't know that banana talk, but I do know you never bring a knife to a gun fight," Tito hissed, then snatched his gun off his waist. Before Smoke could raise the machete Tito had his gun under his chin.

Both of Tito's goons pulled guns and eyed the two dreads across the street.

"Ya nah scare me, yankee bwoh," Smoke laughed. "You gwan shoot, shoot!"

Tito looked around at all the faces, potential witnesses. He itched to splatter Smoke's brains, but he had a better idea. He grabbed Smoke by his locks and dragged him inside the building.

"You fucked up, pussy bwoh!" Smoke laughed madly.

Tito and his goons dragged Smoke up the stairs until they reached the roof. It was then that Smoke showed the first sign of worry.

"Wh-what gwan?" Smoke quipped.

Tito put his gun to Smoke's forehead.

"Speak English, motherfucka! This is America! Harlem! My goddamn city! Look at it! Look!" Tito barked.

They were high enough to see all of Harlem.

"Now, you go back downstairs and tell the rest of your fuckin' people this is my fuckin city, seen?!" Tito bassed in Smoke's face.

"Yeah, I tell 'em," Smoke gritted.

"Okay ... but take the shortcut."

Before Smoke could register what Tito meant, six strong hands grabbed him in six different places and flung him from the roof like a rag doll!

"What the bum ba — "

Twelve flights later, Smoke landed face first in the street, breaking his neck on impact, his blood squirting out of his ears and mouth. His machete hit the ground a few feet away. Tito looked down on the dreads looking up. There was no turning back. He had declared war on the Jamaicans.

CHAPTER 42

"What you laughin' at?" Tre asked Tito.

They were in Dru Hill Park in Baltimore. A nice breeze blew through, ruffling the soft material of Tito's Armani suit. He had stopped through on his way back from Atlanta, so he told Tre to meet him. They always chose open spaces to talk. Force of habit.

"What the fuck are these young nigguhs wearing these days? Pants tighter than a woman's," Tito said, shaking his head as a young dude with a mohawk, young-ass spring jacket, and skinny jeans walked by.

"These young nigguhs wanna dress like white boys, but back in our day, white boys wanted to dress like us," Tre commented, then chuckled. "Remember when your moms kicked you out in that tight-ass Members Only coat!"

They both laughed at the memory that really brought them together.

"Yeah, that shit was tight," Tito admitted. "I was mad as a motherfucka."

"Yeah, but if she ain't kick you out when she did, she coulda smothered you in the crib, feel me?"

Tito understood.

"True indeed."

They both reflected on the point while three teenage girls walked by, giggling and eyeing them suggestively.

"Few more years, mami," Tre winked as they walked by.

"Then you'll be too old to handle it," one shot back, and they broke out with laughter.

Once they were out of earshot, Tito asked, "What up wit' your man, J?"

Tre shrugged.

"Nigguh solid, yo."

"Would you vouch for him?"

"I just did," Tre replied.

Tito nodded,

"Why? What's good?" Tre inquired. He was thinking that Vee had told Tito about Guy Simmons.

Tito contemplated what angle to bring his point through. He decided to tell Tre most, but not all, of the situation.

"Remember the fight your man had with my little cousin, Ty?"

Tre nodded, all ears.

"I killed his brother."

"Word??" Tre answered, taken aback. "So why that nigguh ain't plug 'em on the spot? Why he let that old dude stop him?"

"'Cause that old dude is both their father."

Tito explained the situation. How Vee worked for Ty, how Vee killed Kev, and how they ultimately found out that Vee was Guy's son. He even told him his name was really Vee, a fact that Tre knew, but he didn't let on.

"Goddamn small world, yo," Tre nodded, the picture becoming crystal clear.

He now understood why Vee wanted to be the one to tell Tito and Ty the informant was his father!

"Wow," Tre said, amazed by the revelation.

"What?"

Tre looked at Tito, then answered, "Nothin."

As badly as he wanted to tell Tito, he had given his word to Vee. He knew now Vee was in a tight spot, so he was giving him the benefit of the doubt.

"The reason I wanted to pour you a drink on this thought is because that's your man, feel me? And I respect your judgment. So matter how this shit play out between them, that's where it stay — between them," Tito told him.

"Indeed, my nigguh. I got you," Tre assured him.

Tito's point was clear to Tre. Tito wanted to make sure Vee didn't get a hanve againsty, unless Tito authorized that hand.

Tito was hedging his bet. Although Ty urged a move against Vee to solidify his takeover of the family, Tito saw another angle.

Despite killing Kev, Guy was keeping Vee close. That point alone was significant. Tito didn't care who ran the Simmons family as long as he could run them. If Vee proved to be the better bet, so be it.

"But yo, this his number. Feel him out yourself. Tell him I gave you the number," Tre told him.

Tre normally wouldn't have given Vee's number

out, but it was Tre's way of putting subtle pressure on Vee to keep his end of his bargain.

Tito plugged Vee's number in his phone.

"But yo, I wanted to holla at you too," Tre said.

"About?"

"Yo, I know how far you went back wit' Sarducci. I know the decision wasn't easy to go against him, but I wanted you to know I appreciated it," Tre said sincerely.

He gave Tito a gangsta hug.

"Yo, Sarducci was a good mahfucka, God bless the dead. But in the end, he made the first move. I just knew he would make it, feel me? I wish it could've been different, but I definitely don't regret the decision," Tito explained.

"True, but I know you lost some connects because of it, so I figured Sarducci's loss can be your gain. I wanna bring you in on the company."

"What, the porn thing? I don't know shit about porn, fam," Tito chuckled.

"Nigguh, I ain't sayin' be in the flicks," Tre laughed.

"I'm sayin' throw your bone in the soup, and we all eat."

"That's what it is then. Good look, fam."

Tito gave Tre a firm shake.

"You already know. And yo, get at Vee ASAP. I gotta feelin' he wanna holla at you too," Tre told him.

They knew.

Even before the twins confronted her, Gloria could already tell they knew. There was no warmth to their greetings, no spirit of love in their presence. Around

Theresa, the twins kept up appearances. But when she encountered them alone, Gloria felt the coldness in their demeanor. She knew it was only a matter of time until the sharks stopped circling and made their move.

So it was no surprise when Asia and Brooklyn came to confront her in the living room of Theresa's brownstone. They purposely waited until Theresa was out getting her hair done. Gloria was curled up on the couch watching Tyler Perry's "Why Did I Get Married." Brooklyn took the remote off the table and cut off the TV.

"I see the two of you finally got up the heart to say what's on your mind," Gloria smirked, sitting up on the couch.

"Oh, believe me, it ain't got nothing to do with heart," Brooklyn replied coldly.

Gloria thought she knew her nieces. She didn't. She thought her nieces were pretty little rich girls. Of course they were feisty and sassy, and she knew they would fight, but they were born and bred in Harlem, so that was far from the case. But she didn't know that they were both killers and both had murder in their hearts.

Asia just sat there looking at Gloria, feeling sick to her stomach but trying desperately to understand.

"How could you?" Asia asked with anguish.

Brooklyn's bravado, Gloria could deal with. But the hurt, anger, and questioning in Asia's tone was harder. Gloria sighed deeply.

"Asia, if you have to ask, there's no way you could ever understand," Gloria replied heavily.

How could you ever explain being a fool if you were the only person who had never been one? How could you explain how love can make you blind and crazy, make you see what isn't there, and make you not see what's right in your face?

There were no words, therefore Gloria couldn't answer.

"You goddamn right we can't understand!" Brooklyn huffed, jumping to her feet, her fury making her pace the floor. "Your own brother?! Your own goddamn brother?! Were you there, bitch?! Was it you that pulled the trigger?!" Brooklyn growled, pointing in Gloria's face.

Gloria shot to her feet.

"Brooklyn, don't put your damn hands in my face. I know you upset but don't push it," Gloria warned her.

Brooklyn cocked her head to the side and hit her with a smile so bright, it looked like a maniac on the verge of mutilation.

"Or what, huh? Or what?" Brooklyn asked with a sweetness that dripped poison.

Twins heave their own language. Asia said something to Brooklyn that Gloria didn't catch, but it made Brooklyn fall back and sit on the arm of the chair, reluctantly.

Gloria eyed Brooklyn a moment longer than sat down, crossed her legs, and smoothed her skirt.

"I cannot tell you how many nights," Gloria's voice trailed off, then she sighed deeply. "No, whateva I went through, I deserve, so it doesn't matter. But I will tell you what happened if you want to know."

"We're listening," Asia replied.

"I found out at your grandmother's funeral, from a family friend. She lives across the hall from Eddie. She told me about the gunshots. The-the man that got shot, what he was wearing." She looked at Asia. "Guy had got shot and had been wearing the same thing. At first I didn't want to know. I didn't want to believe what I knew, but something inside made me confront Guy. I had to hear it from him. Make him say it. At first he was evasive. I knew right then. When I looked in his eyes, I saw the shame, and he told me ... everything."

Gloria dropped her head, rubbed her eyes, and then told them the rest. She told them how Po' Charlie had approached Guy because Nicky Barnes' council was about to go down. How the Italians would only deal with a few remaining members and that Eddie was one of them. She told them that in exchange for eliminating these few, Guy would inherit a heroin kingdom.

It was then that Asia saw the justice in Tito's point. It wasn't only about revenging their father's death, it was about reclaiming that for which he was killed.

When Gloria finished, they all sat quietly for what seemed like an eternity to Gloria. She felt like a prisoner awaiting judgment, waiting to be condemned for what she knew was their right to condemn. But she definitely didn't expect the response she got.

"Auntie," Asia began and mustered a smile, although all she felt was disgust, "you're family. Nothing can change that. We need you to do something for family."

Asia paused for Gloria to speak.

"Go on," Gloria replied evenly.

Daddy died for that connect. We want that connect given to Ty. We know about this dude being Guy's son and killing Kev. It's on you to make sure it's Ty that gets that connect and not Vee."

Gloria shook her head.

"I'm not sure I carry any weight with Guy anymore, especially when it comes to his precious son," she said with disgust just thinking of Vee.

"He must listen to you, Auntie," Asia emphasized. "But either way, we say you gonna kill him yourself," she said, her expression stern.

Gloria looked surprised.

"I-I can't. I'm not a killer," she gasped.

Asia stood up and replied, "Then you die. The choice is yours."

The first law of nature is self-preservation. That was the premise on which Asia's ultimatum was based. It would be either her or Guy. Asia seemed to be saying, if you love him so much that you can't kill him, die for him. But if you love you more, kill for us.

A few moments later, Theresa came in and the whole atmosphere changed. It was like the world took off its mask long enough to show Gloria its real, hideous face, then put back on its mask of smiles. But looking in Brooklyn's eyes, she saw no mask.

Gloria knew if there was anybody she could go to for help, it was the one person she wanted to see the most, but self-preservation was the first law of nature.

⚫⚫⚫⚫⚫⚫

The bone-skinny woman furtively glanced back forth as she crossed the street. The geek of a crack high made her more fidgety than usual as she tried to blend into the shadows of the night.

Her name was Margeret Hardy. She was the youngest of the Hardy siblings. Back in her day, they called her Babygirl.

Now people called her everything but a child of God. She cared only about her next high. Nothing was beyond the limit when it came to her next blast. That's why Hawk Bill had used her.

When Vee told him he wanted to get at Hardy, Hawk Bill put out the word through a neutral source that the Wolf Pack wanted to get in touch with Hardy. Once Margeret got the word, and the incentive of partial payment, she was on it like a blood hound. The word reached Hardy.

"Who the fuck is the Wolf Pack?" Hardy had asked his team.

"Them nigguhs that tried to kill ol' man Guy but got Kev instead," Dro explained, passing Hardy the blunt.

"Yeah?" Hardy answered, inhaling the exotic. His interest was piqued.

Two nights later, he was in the cut watching Margeret. He wanted to make sure no one was around. When he was satisfied, he came out the shadows.

"Auntie, you lookin' for me?" he asked.

"There go my favorite nephew," Margeret chimed, her voice gravelly from years of cigarette smoke.

She tried to hug him, but he mushed her away.

"Yo, who is the Wolf Pack?"

"Big money nigguhs, baby boy, money nigguhs. They hate them goddamn Simmons! Killed that Simmons boy goddamn ass! They some goddamn head bustas!" Margeret explained.

"Fuck they wanna know me for?"

"I don't know, baby, but they do got a number right here." She handed him the paper.

555-1381
Vee

Vee used his real alias just in case Hardy checked up on him, like he knew he would.

"Yeah, a'ight," Hardy said, stuffing the number in his pocket. "This better not be a setup. If it is, bitch, you dead."

"Dead?!" Margeret cackled crazily. "Nigguh, I been dead! Been dead!"

She laughed with total abandonment while Hardy disappeared in the shadows.

●●●●●●

Vee hadn't talked to Tito or Ty about Guy. He knew that would be the first thing Tre would ask him about. The next question would be the one he couldn't answer: why not?

It was a question he couldn't answer for himself. Why hadn't he told them? Beef or no beef, by law he was supposed to pull their coat to the presence of an informant. But he hadn't. He hadn't even confronted Guy.

Maybe he should give Tre the green light to handle it. What concern was it of Vee's anyway? Guy may have been his biological, but he had a father. He loved his mother, but how attached could she be to the nigguh after doing twenty years?

But Vee's pride said no. Whatever was to be done to

Guy would be at his hands. He just didn't know what was to be done.

Vee was buzzed into the studio. It was an old warehouse near the Baltimore Harbor that Tre had renovated for the purpose of shooting adult films. The place was big enough to shoot on twenty sets at a time, but currently, they only had seven fully operational.

"Where Tre?" Vee asked the security guard.

"Set five."

Vee nodded and headed for the set. Vee couldn't front, Tre had been right about the money in porn. Red Light Films was the bull of the industry, not only because of their innovative concepts and all-star lineup, but because of the guerilla-type tactics.

Tre was viewed as the Suge Knight of porn. He was rumored to have been behind the murders of Mr. Man and Sean Allen. Although the rumors were true, no one could confirm a thing. All everyone knew was that most of the big-named porn stars were making deals with Red Light, and several black production companies were quietly going out of business.

Get down or lay down.

Vee saw the red light on over the door, which meant they were recording. He opened the door. Another security guard in the room started to bar his entrance, but when he saw it was Vee, he fell back and gave him dap.

The room was unusually packed. Tre really didn't like a lot of people on the set. "Buy the disk! No free peeks!" he would always say, only half jokingly. But today, everybody's eyes were glued to the set. The guard saw Vee looking around and read his mind.

"Y'all nigguhs just discovered a beast! Bitch about to blow … literally," the guard whispered with a snicker. "Fiyah betta look out."

It was then when he heard it.

When you know a song, love a song, can truly feel a song, it doesn't take but a snippet of that song to recognize it. No one ever forgot their favorite song, no matter how long it's been since they've heard it.

That's what Vee was hearing then. Every woman's song is different and distinct.

The moans or gasps when you hit the right spot, the groans and passionate pants, the total surrender when they cum.

That was what Vee was hearing, but his mind wouldn't let him believe it. He pushed through the throng of onlookers, feelin' like a husband who comes home early only to hear the most sickening sound in the world — sickening because it sounds so sweet.

When he got to the front of the crowd, he was face to face with a combination of profound relief and utter sickness.

"Take this dick, you nasty bitch. You love it, don't you?" the muscular bald-head dude said.

"Yes, daddy," Cat squealed. "Ohh, put your big dick in my ass! I love it in my ass!"

Cat was on all fours on a large, round bed. One dude slid his dick in her mouth while the bald-head dude complied with her wishes and slid his porn-thick dick in her ass. Her pussy creamed up instantly and she ate the other dude's dick like the pro she had become.

Vee was stuck. He was confronted with an image he could neither endure nor resist, so both motivations cancelled each other out. He felt numb, paralyzed, and nauseated, and then his anger began to slowly bubble to the surface.

Cat knew he was there. Almost like she felt the energy he was radiating. There was no shame, no shock, no embarrassment.

She was glad he was there, glad he could see what she had become. To see what her mind had convinced her was his fault, what he made her. The dude spread her ass cheeks and plowed her deeper. Cat looked at Vee, and like a singer on stage, she sang for him. The other dude bust all over her face.

Vee snapped. He shoved the dude aside and grabbed Cat by her hair, only to find out it was a wig. It came off in his hand as she pulled away.

"Get up," he hissed like the steam of a pipe about to bust.

Cat looked at him and laughed in his face, then smeared the cum with her palm and licked it off.

As soon as Vee had grabbed Cat, Tre looked up. "Vee! What the fuck?!"

When Cat's pimp, Angelo, saw Vee grab her, he exclaimed, "Nigguh, get yo hands off my bitch!"

As Vee reached for Cat the second time, Angelo grabbed his forearm. Without hesitation, Vee shot an elbow into Angelo's nose, then followed with an overhand left that caught Angelo dead in the mouth and caused him to crumble him to the floor.

The set exploded with action. Cat jumped up, all claws, and landed on Vee's back. "Don't hit my man!" she yelled.

Angelo's two goons pulled their pistols and aimed

them point blank at Vee, but at the same time, both security guards and two of Tre's gunners pulled their pistols and pointed them at Angelo's goons, point blank. The room was a sneeze away from a blood bath.

Vee slung Cat off his back and eyed the goon closest to him, with his gun in his face.

"Nigguh, shoot! You bitch-ass faggot. Your mother's a dick-suckin' whore if you don't pull the goddamn trigger!" Vee barked.

"And if you do, that dick-suckin' bitch'll be cryin' at yo' funeral," one of the security guards warned the goons.

"Shoot!" Vee taunted him.

Under normal circumstances, the goon wouldn't have hesitated, but these weren't normal circumstances. Not when a bullet from him would be answered by a bullet for him.

"P-put 'em down, G," Angelo ordered as he struggled to his feet, holding his busted up face.

The two goons lowered their weapons. Tre's team didn't.

"Yo, Tre, this how you do business?" Angelo asked with a attitude.

Tre looked at Vee. He had no idea what was going on, but there was no hesitation in holding Vee down.
"It is what it is, my nigguh," Tre shrugged.

Angelo nodded. "Okay, y'all win," he said. "Bitch, get your clothes and let's go," he said to Cat.

Vee didn't know what hurt more, hearing a man disrespect his queen so blatantly or seeing her respond so eagerly. Vee grabbed her arm.

"You ain't goin nowhere," he growled.

Cat tried to snatch away, but Vee grabbed her by the throat.

"Goddamn, Tre, you gonna take my hoe too?" Angelo grilled Tre.

It was then when the recognition hit Tre. He knew who the girl was now.

"Ay yo, Angelo, man get the fuck outta here, yo," Tre replied dismissively.

Tre's team took the goons' guns, then put them all out.

Vee shoved Cat down the back hall. She leaped back to her feet, swinging wildly. Vee leaned away and grabbed her arm, wrapping it around her neck.

"Take yo' fuckin hands off me!" Cat screamed.

Vee shoved her in the dressing room and slammed the door.

He threw a robe at her. She threw it down.

"Put some clothes on!"

"Nigguh, fuck you!"

Vee paced the room in fury. This was a feeling he didn't know or understand. The anguish of a furious pain. Furious because he felt helpless against it. It seemed like his whole world was beginning to crumble. First Guy, then his mother, and now Cat.

The words of Miss Sadie echoed in his mind and a chill ran down his spine.

It's going to cost you everything you love.

"What's the matter, Victor? I thought you missed me." Cat smirked seductively. She opened her arms and came towards him. "Where's my kiss?" she snickered, knowing her mouth was caked with another man's cum.

Vee backhanded her so hard he drew blood. But Cat had always been a fighter. She came straight back at him, only to get mushed into the dressing table so hard she broke the mirror. Vee grabbed her by the throat and raised his fist. But he hesitated.

"Go 'head and do it! Do it, Victor! That's all you know how to do anyway is hurt, kill, destroy! Kill me like you killed Taheem!" she cried hysterically.

Her words made Vee stagger as if they were a physical blow.

"Kill … Taheem?!" he echoed in anguish. "What the fuck—"

"You walked away! I called you, Victor! I begged you not to go, but you left me!" Cat screamed.

"I-I-I just wanted to protect …" he began to say, when the irony of the situation hit him. He had sent Cat and Taheem to Baltimore to protect them, but instead, he had sent them to their destruction.

It will cost you …

The anger disappeared and Cat was Cat again. Her raw emotions were vulnerable to the moment she was reliving.

"You knew I was tired. I asked you just to watch Taheem," she began, wrapping her arms around herself, looking at Vee but not seeing him. "I told you, Victor. The pool … the pool. I was tired. But you wouldn't listen and turned away. You said, "You watch him,' and you walked out. Just turned and walked out."

As she told the story, Vee started to understand, and the horror of the realization almost brought tears to his eyes. Cat's mind was fused reality with an abstract form of reality. In reality, Vee had left them in Baltimore but in Cat's mind, the fact that he left became a physical act of his leaving. In her mind, Vee had really been there the day Taheem died, and the way she remembered it was just her worst nightmare making as an illusion of physical form.

Everything you love ...

Vee now knew the meaning of her hatred. She really thought he had been there. She sobbed quietly, holding herself. Vee moved towards her but she pushed him away. The cloud was back in her eyes. The defenses were back up. The old Cat, the Cat he knew was gone, and he would never see that Cat again. He eyed her momentarily, then said, "I'm takin' you back to Raleigh to your parents."

Cat laughed in his face.

"No, you not, because I'm not goin'."

"You don't have a choice," he replied firmly, throwing her another robe.

"Yes, I do. I'll just come back. I'm not leaving Angelo," Cat said, tossing him in Vee's face.

It was a small slap compared to the rest, so he brushed it off and replied, "Then maybe Angelo will leave you."

Cat stepped up closer and spoke slowly and clearly.

"And if he does—if you take him from me like you took Taheem, I swear on Taheem's grave, I'll kill you myself."

Vee could see in her eyes she was dead serious.

"Angelo was there for me when you weren't. He took me in when you left me nowhere to go. I love

Angelo, and you better know, if you kill him, you kill me," she concluded.

Vee nodded, but inside he was boiling.

"You want him, go to him."

Cat didn't hesitate to dress and leave. Vee headed straight to Tre's office. He found him and Fiyah inside talking. Before Vee could say anything, Tre said, "Yo, Vee, that's my word, my nigguh, I ain't know. I ain't even rec—"

Vee cut him off and started spazzing.

"Nigguh, how you ain't know?! I fucking told you! I told you that was my baby mom!"

"When?" Tre shot back.

"When?! That night when I came back from New York! The night of the explosion!"

Tre shook his head. "My word, yo, if you did, I musta forgot. I mean, I know that's your baby moms, but, fam, I lost my man that night. Do you really expect me to remember anything else??"

Vee didn't reply because he knew Tre had a point. He really didn't blame Tre; he just needed to flip on someone and being it was their spot Vee found Cat in, Tre was the most obvious choice.

"So what's up, yo? You wanna push a button on a nigguh?" Tre questioned.

"Naw, yo, I'ma handle it."

Vee headed for the door.

"Yo, Vee. I talked to Tito. I gave him your number. That's peace?"

Vee knew what Tre was getting at, but his mind was elsewhere.

"Yeah, yo, just let me handle this a'ight? After the

film festival, I'll take care of that," Vee replied, then left.

Tre could see Vee was stressing, so he let it go. But there was no question in Tre's mind—after the film festival, Tito would be told one way or the other.

⬤ ⬤ ⬤ ⬤ ⬤ ⬤

Ty pulled up to the ranch and got one of his brand-new BMW 650i convertibles. It had a metallic silver shine to it that made it almost as reflective as a mirror. It looked like he was driving a $100,000 car made of glass.

It had been an impulse buy while he was in ATL, and he was already bored with it. Ty was tired of the toys. What he wanted was power, and for this he had come to Guy to conclude the plan Debra had put in motion. It would be more subtle, but no less diabolical.

"Hey, Pop!" Ty smiled, finding Guy out by the pool. He gave him a hug.

Looking in Guy's face, he could see wrinkles that weren't there before, hair that was once black was now gray.

The realization saddened the son in Ty but thrilled the greed in him at the same time.

"What's going on, boy?"

Sorry I missed your birthday party, Pop. Just trying to cross all the T's and dot all the I's, feel me?" Ty quipped, and the tone he used made Guy realize he was using the old saying to refer to the spelling of Tito's name.

Guy was really relieved Ty didn't come, being that Vee was there.

"But you got at least another 50 birthdays left in ya, old man," Ty joked.

Guy chuckled.

"Whatever the good Lord see fit to give me."

Shantelle walked out on the patio with a drink in each hand. Ty had to do a double take. Shantelle reminded him of the comedian Sommore with her short cut, dark complexion, and thickness. Shantelle's waist was just thinner and ass twice as phat, making her two-piece look delicious.

"Oh, I didn't know we had company, Guy," she said, subtly chiding Guy. She handed him his drink, then slipped on her robe.

"Yeah, baby, my fault. This is my son, Tyquan."

Ty shook her hand.

"Nice to meet you," he said.

"I've heard a lot about you," she said.

They were still shaking hands when Guy said, "Ty, this is Shantelle," he began, then paused long enough to decide to hide the rest, "Vee's mother."

Shantelle felt Ty's grip go limp. She smiled to herself and slipped her hand out.

Ty glared at Guy. Guy casually sipped hisdrink but didn't look at Ty.

"I'll let you two talk," Shantelle said, breaking the silence.

She disappeared inside, beyond the patio door.

When she was good and gone, Ty spoke.

"His mother, Pop? Really?" Ty stressed.

Guy wasn't a man who felt he needed to ever explain himself, but he knew Ty deserved an explanation. He set his drink down and looked at Ty.

"I've known Shantelle for a long time, longer than I

knew your mother, God rest her soul. She's a good woman, and I enjoy her company."

"And what about her son? He good company too? Is that why you came with him to New York?" Ty asked in an accusatorial tone.

Guy controlled his temper.

"Ty, let it go. Okay? Victor isn't a father," Guy replied.

Ty could see Guy's temple flexing, so he knew not to push it. He switched gears and got down to the point of his visit.

"I'm sorry, Pop. It's just … it threw me for a loop comin' here and seein' all this. And I know Vee is your … son. But, Pop, there's no doubt in my mind he was behind that hit on you."

Guy looked at him, and Ty could see the pain in his eyes.

"Because of that Hardy thing?"

Ty shook his head.

"I think I found the girl he used to set you up," Ty told him.

"Who?"

He had Guy's total attention.

"Vee's baby mother, Cat," Ty replied simply.

Guy shook his head.

"Are you sure?"

"Only Karrin can tell us for sure."

Guy eyed Ty.

"Why Karrin?" he asked suspiciously.

"Because Karrin and Cat are cousins. That's how me and Vee met.

If anyone knows where Cat is, it's Karrin. That's

why you have to let me know if Karrin contacts you. Don't talk to her. Put her on ice, but find out where she is," Ty emphasized. "I doubt she's involved, but if anybody can get Cat's whereabouts out of her, it's me," Ty winked.

Because Karrin had refused to tell him where she was, Ty didn't know where her head was. Maybe she was ready to break and confess. Ty couldn't have that. He would kill her first. So he wanted Guy to be aware, just enough for Ty's lie and not the real truth.

"Remember, Pop, let me handle her," Ty repeated.

"Nigguh, I heard you the first time," Guy replied with a touch of impatience.

"I'm just sayin', Pop, because you never fall back and let me handle the business on my own," Ty said.

Guy finished his drink and sighed. He knew Ty was right. He was getting old. He was getting tired. Falling back was what he wanted the most. Ty may not have been a Simmons by blood, but he was Simmons by grooming. Besides, he was the only son Guy had left, except for …

"I said okay, Ty, you handle it."

That's all the license Ty needed.

CHAPTER 43

I can't see it coming down my eyes,
So I had to let the song cry.

Vee wasn't the kind to drink and drive. Tonight was the exception as he turned the bottle of Crown Royal back up to his lips.

I'm a man with pride
You don't do shit like that

He never drove with the radio blasting so loudly he couldn't hear his surroundings. Tonight he had the volume maxed out, trying to drown out his own thoughts.

Once a good girl's gone bad
She's gone forever

Cat ...
The yellow line of the highway weaved back and forth, or was he swerving? To Vee, it was the world that

kept shifting, not him. He was headed to Jessup, Maryland, a little spot outside of D.C. Jatiah had gotten Karrin an apartment out there in her name.

Vee pulled into the parking lot of the complex and damn near sideswiped the car he parked beside.

Cat …

Her face flashed before his eyes. It made his heart ache. Then it was replaced with the cum-stained face of earlier.

Vee opened the car door, put one foot out, then stopped and took a swig.

"Cat … goddamn, ma. I fucked up," he whispered. "But I … I can't go back. He won't let me go."

Vee turned the bottle up and finally found what he was looking for: the bottom.

He tossed the empty bottle to the curb. It cracked but didn't break. He got out, leaving the door open, the car still running, and the headlights on. He staggered to the door.

"Yo, Karrin!" he called out loudly, breaking the silence of the quiet community.

He knocked hard, not seeing the doorbell.

"Karrin!"

Karrin came to the door. "Vee, are you okay? Are you … have you been drinking?" she asked, seeing the obvious.

Karrin looked past him and saw the car still running.

"Vee!" she exclaimed in an admonishing tone.

She went and turned the car off and shut the door. She handed him the key and ushered him inside.

"Come on, before one of these crackas call the police," she giggled.

He stumbled inside.

"Fuck the police. I ain't scared of no goddamn police. They need to be scared of me!" he slurred.

Karrin didn't know how to take him because she had never seen him like that.

"You sure you okay?" she snickered awkwardly.

"Yeah, yeah yo," he replied and plopped down on the couch. "I'm Gucci. I'm Louie. I'm all that shit," Vee chuckled.

Karrin laughed.

"I'ma make you some coffee."

"Naw, yo. Fuck coffee. You got any Henny up in here?"

"Yeah," she said, doubting he needed anything else to drink.

"Then bring me that. Bring the whole bottle," he demanded.

She came back with the Hennessey and handed it to him.

"I've never seen you like this," Karrin remarked, sitting down.

Vee took a swig.

"First time for everything, yo."

He offered her the bottle.

"I'm good."

"You gonna let me drink alone?"

"I don't have a glass," she snickered.

"It's in a glass," he whispered drunkenly.

Karrin took the bottle and looked at it, then took a small swig. Her face squenched up and she handed it back.

"I never drank Henny straight. Now I see why," she

said.

Vee's phone rang. He ignored it.

"Aren't you gonna answer it?"

"Naw," he replied, slugging the bottle, then offering it to her.

She shook her head.

"Vee, what's up? I mean, for real, for real. This ain't you."

Vee looked at her.

"How would you know? Huh? Because you know me?" he laughed. "Do you even know yourself? Did you know that your life would make you this?"

His words hit home, but she tried to evade them.

"What are you talkin' about? This what?"

"Drunk."

This time she took the bottle.

The conversation went on. The bottle got lower. Inhibitions got relaxed, walls went down. True feelings got expressed.

"I shoulda never left," he admitted.

"I ain't have a choice," she confessed.

He leaned forward, resting his elbows on his knees and ran his hand over his waves, disheveling them.

"I did it to protect them. They were the only thing that mattered. I did it for them, and now they're gone because I did it," he chuckled in anguish. "Somebody shoulda protected 'em from me."

She heard his words, but in the context of her own dilemma. She thought of Ty. He was her reason, he was why she did it, and now she couldn't go back to him because of the weight of that decision. The road to hell is paved with good intentions.

He looked at her protruding stomach, then looked her in her eyes.

"Who?"

He had never asked her before. He never felt like it was his business. Now it mattered.

She looked away.

"Kev's."

He nodded. It made sense in his twisted life. He had lost one he loved, only to be given responsibility over one he hated. Even if that hated one was his brother.

He placed his hand on her stomach.

"You can't protect them," he said softly.

"I will," she answered resolutely, as if her life depended on it.

Feeling the life within her made him think of Taheem. Looking at her made him think of Cat. What he had, what he lost, what he dreaded to find.

He bent and kissed her stomach.

She hadn't expected it, but she welcomed the warmth it brought.

"Cat," he whispered with the reverence of prayer, "I'm sorry, baby. I'm so sorry," he repeated gripping her shirt. He fell to his knees before her and kissed her bare knees. "I'd give my life to bring him back, bring us back. But my life is not my own," he cried, kissing up her thigh gently.

She softly parted her lips to say no, but his name came out. She thought of Ty. She felt her loneliness, she felt his caress.

He suddenly thought of seeing Cat at the studio, on her knees. He bit her inner thigh. She shrieked from the pain, shocked by the pleasure. She dug her nails into his back, causing him to suck in his breath.

The pain became their motivating factor, the pleasure, their relentless pursuit. He slid her out of her shorts and found her panty-less and wet. Her toes gripped the carpet, his tongue caressed her clit. Her soft sighs urged him on, his hardness drove her wild.

They were two bodies simply loving the one they were with because they couldn't be with the one they loved. Things would never be the same.

⚫⚫⚫⚫⚫⚫

Gloria told Guy she was coming to Raleigh. She knew that he'd meet her. She didn't base it on his love for her, although she knew he truly did in his own way. She based it on the simple fact that Guy didn't like to lose, especially to a woman. He'd never accept that a woman could really leave him, so her reaching out to him stroked his ego and brought him to her, just as she knew it would.

They met at a restaurant in Raleigh. It was the same restaurant where they had taken Kev to celebrate his high-school graduation. She picked it for that purpose, a fact Guy picked up on instantly but didn't admit to when she asked, "Do you remember the last time we were here?"

"Vaguely," he lied, "but I do remember it."

He wanted to see the reason she chose to meet him there.

Gloria didn't respond. To name the symbol would've been to cheapen it, so she replied, "Doesn't matter."

Guy eyed her admiringly. She definitely looked good. Under the touches of gray and subtle wrinkles, she was still the sassy city girl he fell in love with.

"So when are you comin' home?" Guy smirked, after they ordered.

Gloria retorted, "When you come to your senses. But you won't, so I can't."

"Oh?" Guy answered, leaning his elbows on the table. "What senses have I left?"

She looked him in the eyes. He knew. He just wanted her to say it.

Gloria shook her head.

"You're wrong, Guy. You're wrong and you know it. But that's okay. You've been wrong before, and I stood by you. But the one time I ask you to stand by me, you turned your back. Now ask yourself did I deserve that?"

"It ain't about you deserving," Guy began, but stopped as the waiter brought their order.

When he left, Gloria cut in.

"And that's my point! It's never about what I deserve. You might give me a fur, or give me a house, or even a life. I don't regret all our years. For the most part, they were good years. I was happy, but you didn't do it for me, you did it for you! Mrs. Guy Simmons. That's who you did it for, not Gloria," she released, on the verge of tears.

Guy couldn't dent the truth in her words, but he sought to defend himself against her logic.

"How can you say—" was all he got out before Gloria reached across the table and took his hand.

It was time to run her game.

"It doesn't matter, Guy. I know you loved me

in your own way. My point is you always did for Guy, but when does Guy do for us?"

"Us?"

"Your family, baby. We are a family, a dysfunctional family," she snickered, "but a family nonetheless. But this thing with Vee is hurting that. I know that you won't give me what I want. I don't even know if I want it anymore. But it's hurting Ty too."

Guy suppressed a smile because he was beginning to understand.

"How is that?"

Gloria picked at her salad.

"Just don't forget Ty is your son too."

"You think I have?"

Gloria looked him in the eyes.

"Ty ain't Kev, but I love him like a son. He deserves to take this family into its future. You owe it to Kev," Gloria claimed.

Guy nodded. Now he knew why she chose this setting. It was in the name of Kev. It wasn't his debt to her or even Ty she came to collect on. It was Kev's.

But he knew she hadn't acted alone. He had been playing the game too long not to recognize the alignment of forces. He also knew Ty wasn't behind it either. He didn't have the pull or persuasion to enlist Gloria.

But he knew who did.

"I see your point, baby," he conceded for the moment. Then he cleared his throat and changed gears. He looked at his watch. "I didn't plan on going back to the house tonight. What hotel you say you were at?" he asked, subtly licking his lips, confident in his own appeal.

Gloria cracked a dimpled smile. A part of her loved him, a part of her hated him, but both sides would always want him. Her stomach did flips just thinking about that long black dick up in her.

The twinkle in her eye sealed the deal.

"Eat your food, Guy. You look thin. Whoever the bitch is, she damn sure ain't feedin' you," she said.

Nothing else mattered.

Vee sat hunched on the bench, dressed in rags, gripping a half empty bottle of Irish Rose, watching Angelo.

Vee became a stalker. It took him back to the days when he hunted nigguhs to eat. Back when the Wolf Pack were just wolves.

He watched Angelo, minute by minute, hour by hour, tracking his routine for three days.

He followed Angelo even though Angelo thought he was on point to tails. Vee knew how to track like a pro. He knew you didn't follow a mark all at one time. The smart mark could peep that a mile away. The way to track was piece by piece. If the route consisted of A, B, C, and D streets, the first day you follow the mark from A to B streets, then disappear. The second day, you'd be waiting on B Street to see if the mark made a left or right on C Street. On the third day, you waited on C and followed him to D. D meaning dead.

Vee did this because he wanted Angelo to experience the unspeakable. Cat didn't know the deal she made for Angelo's life was a deal with the devil. The worst thing she could do was tell Vee not to kill Angelo.

Now he would suffer until his death.

Vee wasn't doing it because she had chosen Angelo over him. It was painful, but he could live with that. He would destroy Angelo because Angelo had destroyed Cat. Because he had used her vulnerability and her beauty and turned her into something ugly and deformed.

For that he would pay.

On the third day Vee rose out of the bushes around Angelo's crib. He knew he'd be alone because Angelo didn't even trust his goons to know his real headrest, a strength Vee turned into a weakness.

He put in his key. His key turned the lock.

Click.

The cocking of a gun's hammer can be paralyzing if unexpected. Angelo froze.

"B-b-be easy, playboy, I—"

Vee shoved him inside. He shut the door behind him.

Angelo looked up from the floor. His eyes bulged when he saw Vee.

"She ain't here!" he blurted out.

His fear was so thick Vee could smell it.

"But you are," Vee smiled.

He kicked Angelo dead in the face and blood flew from his mouth. Angelo tried to scamper away. Vee grabbed him by his legs and dragged him into the middle of the living room's hardwood floor.

"Please, man, she came to me! I swear, you can have her, man! I swear!"

Vee didn't answer right away. Instead, he pulled out a mid-sized burlap sack, reached in, and pulled out a handful of graveyard dust and began sprinkling it around Angelo.

Angelo watched him intently, twisting his neck damn near in a complete circle to see his every move.

"Man, what you doin?! What the hell?!"

"Exactly," Vee chuckled.

Angelo thought the dirt was some kind of explosive powder, like TNT. He thought Vee planned on blowing him up.

"No, man! Listen! I-I-I got money! Long money! Upstairs man! The combination is—"

"Take off your pants."

"Huh?"

Vee crouched down and put his gun to Angelo's head.

"Take … off … your … pants," he repeated.

"Brah, not that! Anything but that!" Angelo pleaded, crying real tears.

Vee laughed in his face.

"A bitch-ass nigguh would think that," he replied, then punctuated his statement by slapping Angelo with the gun.

Angelo pulled off his pants, leaving on his silk briefs. Vee kicked him in the nuts as hard as he could.

His mouth was open, his back arched, and his head thrown back. No sound came out until he finally exhaled and moaned in trembling anguish. Vee snapped out a barber's straight razor and slashed Angelo across the face, opening his cheek all the way through to the inside of his mouth. He did the same to the other side of his face.

Vee smeared his hand in the blood and began

splattering it around the circle, mingling it with the graveyard dirt as he recited the Psalms, slowly and methodically.

Angelo's conscious mind didn't grasp it, but his soul did.

"N-n-no … no, please, God … no," he prayed in pain.

The last cut was the worse. Vee slashed Angelo's briefs and grabbed his nuts. Angelo feebly tried to protect himself, but he was still enthralled by the pain of the kick. Vee grabbing and gripping his nuts made the pain more intense.

He was helpless as Vee put the straight razor to his nuts and sliced them off.

The pain was unbearable but not enough to make him pass out. Vee tossed his testicles on his chest, recited one last Psalm then said, "Eat them or die."

Through pain-tinted eyes, Angelo looked up at a madman.

Vee was covered in Angelo's blood, holding a gun. His whole body shuddered.

"Just … just kill me," Angelo gasped.

"Okay," Vee replied and raised the gun.

He knew Angelo didn't mean it. He had seen death wishes in men's eyes, and Angelo didn't have one.

"Wait," Angelo croaked, holding up a feeble hand. "O-okay."

Vee lowered the gun and began reciting again.

Angelo took his testicles in his trembling hand. They were bloody balls of meat that resembled the wrinkled flesh of a newborn puppy.

He looked at Vee. "Why, man?"

"Because you don't want to die like this. That I promise you," Vee warned.

Angelo closed his eyes, put his testicles in his mouth and chewed. Every bite sent a wave of pain through the area his testicles used to be in. Every bite took him closer to the edge.

Vee peeled off his outer garments. Underneath he had on another outfit. He put his clothes in the burlap sack with the rest of the graveyard dirt that would get buried. He put on a pair of latex gloves. He got Angelo's phone off his pants and dialed 911. He laid the phone down outside the circle. He knew they would track it through the GPS. He looked down at Angelo balled up within the circle of death.

His eyes were glassed over. He was mumbling. They weren't words; he was speaking in tongues. Cursed tongues. Unintelligible tongues. He had experienced the unspeakable and would suffer silently until the mercy of death came to claim him.

Five Months Earlier

He watched it like a movie. Like his favorite movie. All six minutes of it. He had memorized it almost down to every gunshot.

Franklin rewound it again. For the past three weeks, he had been spending his evenings the same way, just him, the mall surveillance tape, and an endless stream of coffee. The tape told him a lot. The tape told him nothing. It answered questions but also made him question some answers. He now knew where Banks had gotten the car. He watched him get in and watched Rome run up to the car, only for Asia to blow Rome away.

Franklin even made a score sheet to keep track of who was on who's side:

Kevin Simmons deceased
Michael "Mike G" Grant deceased
Thomas "Dino" Frazier deceased
Tony "Rome" Sanders deceased
Female shooter (unknown) escaped
Dion Banks deceased
Male shooter (Tyquan Simmons?) escaped
Male shooter (unknown) escaped

Five deceased, three escaped.

"The deceased are winnin'," he quipped with a frustrated chuckle.

Then came the questions.

If Ty ran the Wolf Pack, why was he shooting out with them? A power struggle? A ghetto coup? And if Ty and his people were against the Wolf Pack, why did Tony "Rome" Sanders try to kill Banks? And why did the unknown female shooter stop him? Whose side was Banks on? Whoever's side it was, Franklin knew the other side definitely left him slumped over in the parking lot.

Franklin paused the tape. He looked at the five pictures of the deceased. Some were mug shots, some were drivers' licenses. He studied Ty's mug shot. Every angle. He unpaused the tape. He watched who he assumed was Ty run up to where Kev had just been dropped.

"I know that's you, Ty," Franklin mumbled, but he couldn't be sure. Most of the faces weren't conclusive. He had only matched the deceased with the ID and the ID with the person on the screen. That's why the female (Asia) and the two males (Ty and Vee) were unknown.

Franklin sat back on the couch and took a deep breath. He sipped his coffee. "Whatever happened between Ty and the Wolf Pack, Banks was the link — or the break," he surmised.

Thinking of Banks made him automatically think of Banks slaughters. It was bad enough that so many young black men were dying and helping each other to die, but it was tragic when the blood of the innocent was used to make a point. Franklin was determined to make a point of his own. He wouldn't have to wait long.

Three days later, he had one of the killers in custody.

"Well, Franklin, I've got good news and I've got bad news. Where should I start?" Detective Sergeant Randall told him as he propped up on the edge of Franklin's desk.

"I'm a fan of happy endings," Franklin grinned.

"Okay, bad news first. You owe the Feds one," Randall began.

"Then I assume the good news is what I owe them for."

Randall gave him the wink and tooth clinch.

"Bingo. Interrogation room one. Guy named Jerome Mason, A.K.A. Silk ... or Slick ... something slimy," Randall chuckled. "He's a Fed stoolie. They delivered him this morning. Says he has vital info on the Wolf Pack."

Franklin all but jumped out of his seat. As they walked, Randall talked.

"The guy's a mid-level heroin dealer originally from New York. His arrest record reads like a busy calendar until about three years ago. Then all of a sudden he was Mary mother of Jesus."

"When one hand starting washing the other, Fed style, huh?" Franklin guessed.

Randall nodded.

"The feds aren't too keen on exposing their privates. Why now?" Franklin wanted to know.

"Maybe they've become generous exhibitionists," Randall chuckled.

The fact was the Feds were neither generous or exhibitionists.

They were only the middle men. Guy Simmons was the initiator.

It was Guy who had used his leverage with the feds to get the ball rolling against Vee and the Wolf Pack. Silk was just the fall guy. The guy who made other guys fall.

Franklin and Randall walked into the small interrogation room. Silk was sitting at the small metal table, smoking a cigarette.

"Put it out," Franklin told Silk evenly as he sat down across from him.

"Come on, man, I thought you'd want to make an exception for me," Silk winked, like a man who thought he was holding all the cards.

He started to hit the cigarette, but Franklin smoothly plucked it out of his hand and crushed it under his heel.

"It's Detective Franklin, not man, and I don't make exceptions. Now, what can you tell me about the Wolf Pack I don't already know?" Franklin probed.

Guys like Silk made Franklin sick. On the surface, they thought they had it all figured out, all smooth and tough acting. While underneath they had the heart of a roach. A measly little scavenger surviving off scraps and living in unreliable cracks.

"Be easy, detective. I'm here of my own accord. I'm just doin' my civic duty, you know? All I'm askin' is a little mutual understanding," Silk drawled, then cracked a gold-grilled smile.

Franklin knew exactly what Silk was trying to do. He was trying to use the information he had as a hedge against a future debt. A get-out-of-jail-free card with the state, like he had with the Feds.

Franklin got up.

"Sarge, I guess we can tell Mr. Mason's feed pimp that their ho won't swallow," Franklin smirked.

Silk bristled at the comment.

"Yo, watch you goddamn mouth. I ain't nobody's ho," Silk seethed.

Franklin's reply was a smile. He turned to leave, calling Silk's bluff.

A split second was all it took for Silk to fold, or in Franklin's words, swallow.

"Okay, man — I mean, detective. I'll tell you what you wanna know."

Franklin sat down.

"Whenever you're ready."

"It's about the murders."

"What murders?"

"That nigguh Banks' family, yo," Silk said.

Franklin was all ears.

"What about it?"

Silk sighed hard and shook his head.

"Look, man, this some real shit. And them Wolf Pack nigguhs?" Silk shook his head again. "All I'm sayin' is at the end of the day, who gonna be there for me?"

"Call 911. We'll be there as soon as we can," Franklin said matter of factly.

Silk sucked his teeth. Franklin continued.

"I'm not here to hold your hand. I'm not concerned with your safety. I am only concerned with solving this case. Are we clear?"

Silk eyed Franklin hard. He knew he couldn't disobey his Federal masters, so he replied, "The dudes that did it were little nigguhs with the Pack."

"Explain."

Silk shrugged.

"Little nigguhs, yo. Young boys wit' something to prove. The type willing to do whateva so the big dogs know they go hard."

Franklin nodded.

"You got names."

"Yeah, I got names. I ain't saying they did it for sure, but I guarantee they know who did it. Lil' Man, Boo, and Killa."

Franklin wrote.

"No real names?"

"Naw, but they be out in west Durham, in the projects."

"Could you ID 'em?"

"I could, but I ain't," Silk replied indignantly. "Ain't no goddamn way."

Franklin could taste the justice. He knew he was close, real close. He couldn't let that get away.

"Okay, look, you do this for me," Franklin said, flexing his jaw muscle, "and I won't forget it. You have my word."

Silk knew this was the only bone Franklin would throw. He jumped at it.

"Okay ... for you," Silk replied.

It would be Franklin's first introductory step to his last temptation.

"One other thing," Franklin said, pulling up a picture on his phone, then sliding the phone in front of Silk. "Can you tell me who he is?"

Silk looked down at the picture, then back up at Franklin, wearing a smile like he had all the sense.

"No doubt. His fake alias is J-love, but I know his real alias. They call him Vee, and he run the Wolf Pack.

Mama need a house
Baby need some shoes
Times is getting hard
Guess what I'ma do

Ace Hood's "Hustle Hard" blared loudly from the speakers, filling the already crowded project living room. Young girls struck poses for young boys oblivious to everything but bravado. Somebody's mama wasn't home, and the crib had become party central.

Fifteen minutes earlier, Silk gave the police a positive ID on Lil' Man and Boo. They had just entered the apartment.

"Everybody ready?"

"10-4."

"Let's rock and roll!"

The raid was lightening fast. Squad cars came from every direction. People ran in every direction. Girls screamed. Police barked. A warning shot went off. The police were quick. Boo was quicker. He slipped past the dragnet. Lil' Man wasn't as lucky.

"Down on the ground now! Don't move!" Franklin bassed, his gun aimed at Lil' Man's head.

"A'ight, man, chill! Chill!"

"Now!"

Lil' Man slowly got to his knees, crossed his feet at the ankles, and laced his fingers behind his head. He knew the routine. Seconds later he found himself with a face full of carpet.

Franklin cuffed him hard.

"Man, what I do?!" Lil' Man gruffed.

Pulling the heroin out of his pocket and gun off his waist, Franklin replied, "You did enough! You have the right to — "

"What do we have here?!"

Franklin turned in the direction of the sound of the dice.

What he saw made him sick to his stomach. An officer held a gun up in one hand and the collar of Darnell, Franklin's young protégé. Their eyes met. Darnell gazed brazenly. Franklin was the first to drop his head.

CHAPTER 44

"Come, Star, come reason with the Dread," Bobo called out to Tre.

Tre and a few members of the team were in front of one of Tre's gates on 171st in the Bronx.

Bobo had pulled up in a blue and gray Granddaddy Benz 600.

He was Tre's connect. But Tre knew this wasn't about the re-up. It was about Tito's beef with the Jamaicans in Harlem. Tre knew once Tito threw Smoke off the roof, Bobo would come check for him. Tre walked up to the car and leaned in the passenger's seat and shook Bobo's hand.

"Peace, Bo."

"Respect, my youth. Come on and get in," Bobo replied.

Tre had his strap on his waist. Still, he knew Bobo was a dangerous man. He was a high-ranking member of the Black Rose Massive, one of the most violent massives to come out of the yard. Tre got in. Bobo put the car in gear.

"Naw, Bo, we good right here."

Bobo smiled knowingly, shrugged, and put it back in park.

"I come in peace wit' the reasonin' of de elders, my youth. Because the Dread understand these tings. It's sipple out deh."

Tre smiled to himself. He knew where Bobo was coming from and where he was going. He knew when Bobo said "sipple out dere," it meant it's slippery, it's dangerous in those streets.

Tre let him continue without commenting.

"Now the Dread, him know dat you a businessman. You young but you smart. Ya nah wan ire dem. But dem-a-say the youth inna 'arlem, im wan be a bad man and that nah good for business, seen?" Bobo explained patiently but firmly, with a smile of conciliation on his face but ice in his eyes.

There was no mistaking the message. Tre made sure there was no mistaking his answer.

"True indeed, Bo, true indeed. But just like you, I wanna do business. But you here now talkin' about war. That's my nigguh, and if that's what you sayin', then fuck it."

"Me nah wan war wit' you. Me nah say that, me say ire dem, ya understand? Ire dem."

"I know, yo, make them mad. I understand."

"He come to you fa peace. Reason wit' your brethren He young. Black Rose big name, long time," Bobo boasted with the bass of bravado.

Tre chuckled. Bobo was telling him Black Rose was the big dog and they were just youngins.

"Yeah, a'ight, Bo. I'll talk to him. But, yo, I'm 'bout dry. I need to see you," Tre said.

Bobo looked straight ahead, his hand draped over the steering wheel.

"Check me back little later eh. A little later."

Tre knew that meant later would never come. Bobo was cutting them off, so in this war, they'd be beaten by attrition."

"No problem, Bo. Peace."

"Respect."

Tre got out and went straight to the phone booth to beep Tito as Bobo pulled off.

Tito didn't even hear his beeper.

The gunshots were too loud.

"Buummm Baaa clllooottt!" The Dread yelled as he rose out the back window of the old Buick and let the moderation begin.

Tito and his team had been coming out of Morningside Park after playing basketball. The Dreads had it planned: While Bobo went to see if he could throw Tre against Tito, or at least neutralize him, the hit team would dispose of Tito. The beef had been basically lopsided. Tito and his people couldn't match the Dreads in gunfire, but they more than matched them in terms of heart. They wouldn't hide, but that just made them easier to kill. Today was to be the final onslaught, but it would ultimately turn the tide.

Two Buicks, four gunmen, all brandishing the newest occupant of the ghetto: the Uzi submachine gun. It was the first fully automatic weapon to hit the hood. The way the Uzi fired, was a menacing combination of sight and sound. Tito and his crew had taped-up .38s and rusty .45s. All they could do as they came out of the park was run for cover. Two of them weren't fast enough.

The Dreads spread the bullets like they were painting the streets. Car windows exploded, triggering alarms, cars screeched to a halt, pedestrians screamed and ducked. It seemed like an eternity but was over in less than a minute. The two Buicks screeched off as Tito fired a few frustrated rounds as they sped away.

"Fuck!" he barked, his energy a mixture of anger, anxiety, fear, and adrenaline.

He saw two of his people lying in their own blood, dead.

He started to go to them but the sounds of approaching sirens changed his mind.

"They gone, T! We didn't save 'em. Let's go!" Sleep exclaimed.

Reluctantly, Tito complied and they all disappeared.

Anger has many forms. You will find that the loudest, most belligerent anger is just blowing off steam. That is the anger of fools. Some anger is mindless madness. That is the uncontrollable anger of insanity. But the quiet anger, the anger that is focused, controlled, and fearless is the anger of power.

Tito possessed the third kind of anger. He, Tre, and Sleep sat in the dimly lit basement of an apartment building, surrounded by the sounds of rats, malfunctioning generators, and muffled voices from the apartments above them. The only light was the swinging bulb dangling just above their heads and the glowing tip of Sleep's cigarette.

"So you in or not?" Tito asked Tre, looking him in the eyes.

Tre shook his head. "This shit is crazy, B! Fuckin' suicide! I love you like a little brother, Tito, but goddamn! We got fuckin' seven guns between us."

"Six," Tito corrected him. "Mark had the chrome .380 on him when he died."

Tre sighed.

"That's my point! We might as well say fuck it and go at these nigguhs with bass and chains! That's the only thing we got more than them!" Sleep nonchalantly blew out the smoke.

"I'm wit' it."

Tre looked at Sleep. He and Sleep went way back. He had sent Sleep to hold Tito down in Harlem and teach him how to run a weed gate.

"Yo, how much them shits cost? Them guns they had?" Tito asked.

"Like a grand a piece, maybe a little more," Sleep replied.

"I got fifteen G's stacked. That'll get us fifteen," Tito said, looking at Tre.

Tre knew that was probably Tito's whole stash.

"T, word is bond, I know the cut of your cloth, but I told you, Bobo cut us off! We ain't got no connect, period! You spend your last, then what? This shit is suicide!"

"If it is, fuck it. I'd rather be dead than fold my goddamn hand! What do it matter? If we lose, we deserve to die! I ain't just talkin' about the Dreads; It could be anybody! If we ain't that nigguh to them nigguhs out there, we ain't got no business in this game. Shit, you say this is impossible, maybe it is. If so, everything else after this will be easy," Tito jeweled him.

Tito couldn't front of Tito's point. He not only understood, he felt it.

The shit was so real, Tre's only response was a handshake.

"Just put up ten, and I'll match it, Uzi for Uzi," Tre joked, using a Jamaican accent.

Their collective laughter broke the tension.

The Dreads had written Tito and his team off. They were young boys they had to teach a lesson. They lost a few men, but they were only pawns, Smoke included. But they had run Tito off of the block. That's what Tito wanted them to think. Confidence can be made a weakness if it exceeds its limit. They underestimated Tito, their first and last mistake.

Gun Hill Road in the Bronx was the Dreads' stronghold. This is where they ate, slept, and partied. They were deep with guns, big guns. They never expected anyone to be foolish enough to try and hit them on Gun Hill.

The plan was simple. One team of dudes would rush the front of the building, another team would hit the back. Each team consisted of seven people, and everyone had an Uzi. Tito,

Sleep, and Tre would creep from roof to roof to take the Dreads from the top. They each had two Uzis.

The two seven-man teams were really just a diversion.

Tre knew they were sending them on some kamikaze shit.

"Them nigguhs will never make it in the building," Tre surmised.

Tito had shrugged.

"Fuck 'em! Use nigguhs you don't give a fuck about."

Tre knew Bobo's layout of the stash house, his lay up and where he kept the pounds. The diversion would draw the fire while Tre, Tito, and Sleep slipped in like shadows.

They came over three roofs that were basically connected.

When they reached the Dreads' building, Tre checked his watch. The two teams were to set it off at the same time: 7:30. It was 7:23.

"Go hard or go home."

"Go hard."

"Let's make a movie!"

Tito glanced down and saw a van pull up. Six white men got out carrying ladders and gallons of paint.

"Yo, Tre," Tito said, then motioned with his head to look down.

Tre and Sleep looked.

"Who the fuck paints at night?" Sleep asked suspiciously.

"You think the Dreads under surveillance?" Tre questioned.

Tito checked his watch. 7:29.

"No turning back now."

Collective shrug. A chorus of cocking Uzis. Seconds later, the sound of several automatics barked as one and was rapidly followed by corresponding barking replies. Tito, Tre, and Sleep went down the fire escape to the top landing and kicked in the window.

They crept to the next floor. They looked down the steps and could see hands holding guns descending the stairs. They heard the sound off rapid-fire.

By the time they reached Bobo's floor, the shooting abruptly stopped. The echo of the last ricochet was all that reverberated. The three looked at each other. They tensed up as they turned into Bobo's hallway.

It was a blood bath.

Dead Dreads, five in all, lay in various chalk line–ready positions, their brains, guts, and last bowel movements still dripping from the ceiling and oozing on the floor. They all had the same thought: Maybe the two-team diversion was better than they thought!

Tre pointed to the open apartment doors. It was Bobo's stash spot. The three of them had their Uzis ready and entered the room cautiously. The first thing they encountered was a dead naked female, still twitching. Down the hall lay Bobo's body, wearing only Speedos, and another dead naked female beside him. They looked to the right, through an open bedroom door, and all six of their eyes got big. The room was stacked with hefty bags full of weed! The pungent odor of the weed hit them like a breath of fresh air.

"Nigguh, I love you for makin' me do this!" Tre laughed.

Someone behind them cleared his throat. They all whirled quickly, raising their Uzis.

It was one of the painters, carrying a sawed-off shotgun. Then they heard movement behind them. Two more painters carrying big guns stepped out of the back bedroom.

"Don't shoot," the lead painter chuckled. "We're wit' you guys."

"What?!" Tito stressed, but he felt no threat because no guns were aimed at them.

"Permit me to explain later. I think it's best we get outta here."

"What about all that?" Tre asked greedily, referring to the weed.

"Leave it. It makes for a better point.."

"Who are you?"

"Vinnie, Vinnie Sarducci. I'm Vito's nephew. He sent me. He told me to tell you, 'When the student is ready, the teacher will come.' Now can we go?" Vinnie smirked.

And they went ... straight to the top.

⬤⬤⬤⬤⬤⬤

Ty got out of the passenger's side of his block captain's Escalade with an arrogant smirk on his face and extra bop in his swag.

He was in Durham, back in the hood, back in his element.

Ty hadn't really re-established any kind of presence on the streets since he had been home. He kept layers between himself and the streets like a boss is supposed to.

But Hardy had changed all that. Since Hardy had come through all Ty's spots like a hurricane of death and destruction, Ty was making his rounds, letting all know he wasn't hiding.

Ty had a point to prove. Now that he knew for sure that Hardy had killed his mother, he had to find him and pull the trigger himself. Ty felt responsible. He had the dude in his grasp and he let him slip away. Until Hardy was dead, bloody at his feet, Ty wouldn't rest. Both were determined to find the other. It was only a matter of time.

"What up, my dude!"

"Long time no see!"

"Yo, I ain't know you was out!"

That was the chorus of greetings Ty received as he entered his barbershop, T.S. (Ty Simmons) on Fayetteville Street, just down the block from Central University.

Ty jumped into thea chair and his top barber covered him with a smock. He looked like he had just gotten out of a barber's chair; his edge-up was still razor sharp, but he wanted the barber to freshen it up.

Small talk about prison and freedom evolved until they got to the topic he came for.

"Yeah, Ty, whoever that nigguh is did Melo dirty, my dude, real talk. They say he blew his baby girl away, raped him and his baby mama, then popped they top," the barber told him.

He didn't mention the other part because he didn't know how Ty would take it, but Ty already knew. It was the same after every murder. Hardy would call every number in the deceased person's phone asking for Ty. When he found out it wasn't Ty, he would leave a message like, "Tell that bitch-ass nigguh he gonna suck my dick just to beg me to kill him! This young Hardy. I did it!"

Everywhere Ty went he caught the questioning glances of dudes. The streets were watching. They knew Ty went hard, but seeing Hardy's work, they wondered if Ty was willing to go hard enough. Ty was there to let the hood knew he was.

"Fuck that faggot, yo. I ain't hard to find. I'll be in Lonzo's tonight. And I got a hundred large on that nigguh head to any nigguh let me know where he at," Ty announced.

Almost on cue, Silk walked in.

"Hundred large?! Can't nobody play wit' numbers like that accept my nigguh, Fly Ty," Silk greeted, approaching the chair.

Ty knew Silk through the block captain he was riding with. He also knew that Silk was one of Vee's main customers.

Ty greeted Silk like he really gave a fuck about him.

"What up, Silk? How you?" Ty smiled, giving him a firm pound.

"Not as good as you," Silk replied, eyeing Ty's jewels. "Goddamn, Ty, if I had your hand, I'd throw mine in."

Ty shrugged. "They all winnin' hands if you play 'em right."

Ty got out the chair, then he, his block captain, and Silk went outside.

"So what's really good, nigguh?" Ty questioned.

"You know, yo, just trying to touch something. Pour me a drink," Silk threw back.

"I'm sayin', I thought you was drinkin' wit' my nigguh Vee?" Ty questioned.

"Man, that nigguh done. You ain't heard?"

"Naw."

Silk told him all about the Banks family murder, how the Wolf Pack was under investigation and how one of the killers was locked up awaiting trial.

"Listen, my nigguh, if you hear from Vee, tell him get at me. Tell him I'm home," Ty said, giving Silk his number.

"Fo' sho'," Silk assured him, pocketing the number like it was a thousand-dollar bill.

"Make sure," Ty emphasized. "Vee don't know I'm out. So if he on the run, I got him."

"What about me?" Silk chuckled as Ty and his man got in the Escalade.

Ty paused in the opened door.

"I been layin' since I touched. But when I make a move, you'll be the first to know," Ty lied.

"Fo' sho'!" Silk replied, but he had all the payment he needed. As soon as the Escalade bent the corner, Silk was on his phone. It went straight to voicemail.

"Yo, Franklin, this your man Silk! Boy, have I got news for you!"

"Yo."

"Who the fuck is this?"

"You called me. Who you lookin for?"

"Vee."

"No names, yo. This a burnout but you never know."

Pause.

"I got your message."

"I see."

"So what you want wit' me?"

"It ain't you I want. We just want the same thing. Problem is, I know how, but I ain't got the soldiers. You got the soldiers, but you don't know how."

"How you figure I don't know how?"

Because you keep missin'."

Pause.

"I wanna see your face."

"I'm in South Beach, Miami."

"I'll hit you when I get there."

Click.

Vee pocketed his and phone and took in the spectacle that is South Beach.

Vee had come for the American Black Film Festival, the ABFR.

It was started in 1997 on behalf of Jeff Friday, one of the power players in the black film industry. Once it moved to Miami in '02, it's prominence and influence took off.

Tre had been in negotiations with Charles Communications, which was on the verge of launching the first black-owned satellite TV network. Tre wanted to get in on the ground floor and secure the primary porn interest in the new venture. The only reason he hadn't come was because he was in Canada, expanding Red Light Films distribution in that country. Therefore, Vee had to handle the situation alone, a role he wasn't used to, but he knew enough about the deal to be able to handle this stage of negotiations.

His wasn't the only familiar face at the festival.

"Ms. Charles, Ms. Charles, do you think the African-American market is sufficient enough to support a billion-dollar satellite network?" The Chinese female journalist asked.

Vanya smiled graciously, like an adult at the naivety of a child.

"First of all, because it will be black owned doesn't mean it will be black only, although it will be black oriented. Secondly, the African-American market contributes over a billion dollars a year to our economy, and as a producer, adds quadruple that to our G.N.P. I see no reason why a market that substantial should be any less sustainable than a white-owned venture. Next question."

Vanya Charles stood in the lobby of the hotel, surrounded by cameras and reporters, holding court like a queen in a fuchsia and blue skirt suit. She was beautiful and powerful. The color of French vanilla, the full-bodied curvaceousness of Jennifer Hudson 27.0, and an uncanny resemblance to LisaRaye, Vanya was sexy as hell. "Ms. Charles, will you show videos?" a middle-aged white reporter asked blankly.

She mentally rolled her eyes, then answered with a straight face, "Of course, 24/7 around the clock, sponsored by Kentucky Fried Chicken and Cadillac.

The group of reporters broke out laughing. The white dude turned red with embarrassment.

"Ms. Charles, I want to compliment you on your family's endeavor, your intuitive mind, and mind-blowing reality, but would you say, despite all this, that success is nothing without a black man to share it with?"

All eyes turned in the direction of the deep voice to find it belonged to man who was black, tall, and handsome.

It was Tito.

Vanya smiled and replied, "No, that would be Billy Dee in the movie 'Mahogany.' And yes, we do plan on having a retro channel," she quipped.

Vanya dismissed the media after two more questions, then she and Tito hugged.

"I like the way you handled that cracka," Tito complimented her.

Vanya rolled her eyes.

"Please. What I really wanted to tell him we're going to show is rap videos, baby-mama drama, and a documentary on all white men's little dicks."

Tito laughed.

"I know that's right. Listen, I just stopped through to see you. I've got a meeting with Jimmy Iovine in twenty minutes. Did you look over that proposal?" Tito asked.

Vanya nodded.

"I like the premise. When can I see it fleshed out?"

"Soon."

"Okay."

"When can I see you fleshed out?" Tito winked with a lip-biting smile.

Vanya couldn't help but think of the last time she had seen Tito. In Atlanta. When dinner turned into breakfast. She smiled to herself. She liked Tito's swag, not to mention his tongue game, but Tito was pursuing more than her, he was pursuing her name. He was ambitious, which Vanya always required in a man, but she wanted more. Besides, Vanya liked to be free. She was Zane freaky but queen classy and had the ability to detach sex from emotion like men.

"Soon," she replied flirtatiously.

Tito smiled.

"But never soon enough for me, sweetness," he answered, kissing her sensually on the cheek. "I'll call you after the meeting."

Meanwhile, Vee was at an outdoor restaurant, nursing a

too-sweet drink, talking to a rep from Charles Communications, the type of young black man who prided himself on having no swagger, a la Tavis Smiley.

"Don't get me wrong, Red Light Films is definitely making its presence felt in the adult-film world, but I'm not sure that it would be the right ... fit for what we have in mind," the rep said.

Vee set the drink down and left it untouched.

"I don't see why not, being that most of the major black names in porn can't make a move without us. Either they signed to us exclusively, we manage them, or a non-competition gives us the right to dead any deal wit' us," Vee concluded.

"Yes, but it is exactly your tactics that concern us," the rep replied cautiously. "Certain ... rumors, you understand, have reached that ..."

Vee's mind blocked out the rep for two reason. One, he knew what he was saying: Charles Communications doesn't deal with gangstas. But Vee knew they would have to deal if they wanted a black porn presence in their satellite.

The second was the sexy, confident strut of the woman walking in their direction. She wasn't fat by any means, but she was definitely country thick. But she didn't use her clothes to flaunt it, only to accentuate it. It wasn't so much an attraction for Vee, it was just admiration of a woman unafraid to exude confidence. He was surprised to see her approach their table.

"Sorry, I'm late. The press conference ran a little long, Rob. I'm Vanya Charles. And you are?" she asked, noting how fine Vee was. She extended her hand and Vee shook it.

"I'm Vee."

Rob pulled out her chair as she sat.

"Thank you. Vee? Is that with two E's or just V?" she quipped sarcastically but playfully.

Vee smiled. He forgot in this world you gave names, not aliases. So he hedged.

"Victor, Victor Braswell," he replied, using Shantelle's last name.

"Nice to meet you. Where's Tradero?"

"He had to handle something."

"Oh, so I take it Canada is a go," she smirked, letting him know she knew the answer already.

Vee shrugged. "Somethin' like that."

"I see," she replied as she pictured Vee naked.

It was lust at first sight for Vanya, not because of Vee's street appeal or any bad-boy fetish she had; she simply wanted him. He seemed to have the quality of a caged panther, but only caged by its own discipline. The whole filmy decadence of South Beach seemed timid as his backdrop. The thought made her curl her toes in her shoes. Rob suddenly he felt...unnecessarily he cleared his throat to reassert his presence.

"Yes, well, I was just telling Mr. Murphy I don't think —"

"Exactly, Rob. You don't think. Victor, please excuse Rob. His position with the company demands him to be conservative. I don't have such restraints," Vanya smiled suggestively. "But there are a few things that concern me."

"Like?"

Like whether or not you have plans tonight, and if we can discuss the rest of my concerns over dinner,"

Vanya just looked at him.

Vee couldn't help but laugh. He liked her style, her self-assured feminine aggression.

"Naw, ma, no plans."

Vanya wrote down her number and slid it across the table to Vee.

"Do you know this restaurant?"

"I'll find it," Vee assured her.

"Eight o'clock? Just ask for the Charles' table. I have standing reservations," she said, in a tone void of bragging.

"Must be nice," Vee cracked.

"And it gets greater later," she winked as she got up.

Vanya exited the patio. Vee watched her as she left.

Later that evening, Vee pulled up to the valet at the Blue Door, an all-black Ferrari Testarossa.

Tre had rented the car in the company's name, so Vee just decided to put it to use.

He entered the restaurant and instantly recognized several faces from films and music. He made his way to Vanya's corner table to find her in the company of a well-known actress. When Vee arrived, Vanya made the introduction, then the actress sashayed away.

"How you doing, Victor? Or should I call you V?" she asked jokingly.

He shrugged. "Victor's cool."

Before Vanya could reply, two more well wishers came by. A famous black director who seemed to be speaking from his knees in her presence and a very gay black TV actor whom Vee found amusing. Then a bottle of Veuve Cicquot arrived, compliments of the house. Vee popped the cork and filled both of their flutes.

"Wow, man, I'm scared of you. You must be like a don, huh? Vee cracked.

"Dona," she winked with a giggle. "No, really, it isn't just me, it's my family. Charles Communications owns many radio stations, newspapers, and television stations around the country. Everybody wants favors." Vee raised his glass.

"Well, to you. To Vanya, without the Charles," Vee toasted, and the sentiment made her smile.

They drank.

"But I'm not the only famous one at the table. I've heard a lot about you too," she said with a smirk.

"Yeah? Do you believe it?"

"Let's just say that I believe that no success comes without struggle. So when they say blood, sweat, and tears, sometimes it takes more of one and less of the others in certain situations," she reasoned smoothly.

"Maybe," Vee replied cautiously.

Sensing his tone, Vanya asked, "Do you know how the Kennedy family got its start?"

"How?"

"Bootlegging. Alcohol, the drug of the twenties, was outlawed during prohibition. All it did is make gangstas rich. Joe Kennedy was one of them. But that's not what you hear because the Kennedys turned money into power. No one remembers the means, Victor, only the ends."

Vee nodded understandingly.

"I agree."

"I always check out the people I do business with, so

I know Tre came up getting his hands dirty. But he paralyzed that, got out of the game, and made his money work for him. I respect that. But I also know that Red Light didn't register until you came on the scene. Just like that. No one knew your name or face until now. So it's good to be able to put a name to such a handsome face," she smiled flirtatiously.

Before Vee could respond, the familiarity of a male voice made him look up.

"What's going on, Vanya? How you doing?" Tito greeted, kissing her on the cheek. He glanced over and pretended he hadn't seen Vee sitting there. "Vee! What's good, my dude? I ain't know you knew Vanya."

"I don't, but I'm getting to," Vanya answered.

"Tre couldn't make it," Vee added, watching Tito watch Vanya.

"That's what's up. But I'm glad to run into you. I'm flyin' out tomorrow, but me and you need to kick it," Tito suggested.

"Fo' sho'. Hit me in the morning."

Tito glanced at Vanya. She met his glance. She could tell he was upset, but he hid it well.

"Okay, Ms. Charles, I see you," he chuckled. "Maybe we can get together on that proposal soon."

He threw the word at her like an accusation, an invitation, and a suggestion all rolled into one.

"I'm looking forward to it," she smiled politely.

Tito glanced at Vee one last time, then walked away. Vanya started to ask Vee how he knew Tito, but their food came and by the time the waiter left, she had decided to let it go.

The night wore on and they got to know each other a

little better.

Vee asked where she was from.

"Boston, as in the Boston Charleses," she answered in a mockingly exaggerated Boston accent. "Not to be confused with our country cousins, the Philadelphia Charleses, as my father called them," she laughed.

"Ain't nothing wrong with being country, yo. I rep N.C.," Vee remarked casually.

"I know. I love country like I love molasses. Dark, sticky, and thick," she flirted.

From then on the conversation became subtly more intimate.

"How honest do you believe in being?" she asked, sipping an after-dinner espresso.

"Depends on the situation," Vee answered.

Vanya giggled.

"Now, that is the most honest I've ever heard!" They both laughed at the irony of truth.

"What if I told you I wanted to sleep with you, no questions asked?" she probed, eyeing him with a twinkle in her eyes.

"Then I wouldn't ask no questions," Vee shot back.

"You sure you can handle that? Most men can't."

"I'm not most men."

"That's why my approach is so direct," Vanya volleyed."

Vee got a text.

I'm here where you?

When Vee looked up from the phone, Vanya saw all the playfulness gone from his eyes.

"I gotta go," he said as he stood up.

"Is everything okay?"

"Yeah."

"Then it can wait."

Vee just looked at her, then walked out. Vanya was heated. No man had ever been that close to her heaven and turned away. The thought irritated her, but the challenge implied by it turned her on.

⚫⚫⚫⚫⚫⚫

Vee turned the Ferrari into the half-filled Wal-Mart where Hardy had told him to meet him. He saw the gray Explorer and parked three spots away. A young dude got out of the passenger's seat. Three more remained in the Explorer.

He approached the Ferrari.

"You Vee?"

"Where's Hardy?" Vee asked without answering because he didn't recognize the voices.

"Get out the car," the dude ordered gruffly.

Vee complied to give the dude the impression he was in control.

"I gotta make sure you ain't strapped."

Vee held up his shirt to reveal he was unarmed. Seeing this, the dude spoke with more bass in his voice.

"Turn around."

"Fuck outta my face," Vee hissed and began to walk towards the Explorer.

The dude attempted to grab Vee's arm. Vee snatched away, grabbed dude by his throat, pinned him against the Ferrari, and grabbed the dude's gun that he had stuffed in the front of his pants. Vee didn't pull the gun out, he just gripped it with his finger on the trigger.

"Now I'm strapped," Vee growled.

The dude clawed helplessly at Vee's vise-like grip. The other three dudes bailed out the Explorer. All Vee heard was barked threats and cocking weapons, then he felt the cold steel of an AK-47, a mini-14, and a riot pump to his head and neck.

"I said let my man the fuck go!" Dro bassed, gripping the pump.

Vee increased the pressure.

"Fuck all y'all," Vee replied, fully committed to the consequences.

The dude's clawing was getting less intense, his movement more lethargic. He was losing consciousness.

A silver Navigator pulled up. Hardy leaned his elbow out the window. He and Vee met in that first glance. Hardy could smell fear a mile away. He smelled none coming from Vee. He knew, rightly or wrongly, Vee was ready to die. That was the ending for him.

"Y'all nigguhs fall back now," Hardy ordered his soldiers.

They complied reluctantly but without delay.

"Next time, nigguh, don't hesitate," Vee schooled the dude, then released his grip.

The dude gasped for air as if he'd been drowning. He leaned against the car, wheezing and heaving, feeling a pounding headache in his temples.

Vee walked towards the Navigator. As Hardy got out, Vee's first impression of Hardy came in one word: thirsty. Not in the normal sense, but in the sense of one ready, willing, and trained to go. He reminded Vee of his younger self.

"Yo, dawg, was all that really necessary? You could got left lonely out this motherfucka over a simple misunderstanding," Hardy remarked with a smirk on his face.

"Yeah, well, at least, now we understand each other," Vee retorted.

"So what is it we think we both want?"

"Ty."

Hardy studied Vee's face and his thoughts turned to Greenville.

The day of Dino's wedding. At that time, Hardy was prepared to kill Vee for the Simmonses. Now he was ready to kill the Simmonses with Vee.

Vee seemed to read his mind through his facial expressions.

"Yeah, I know," Vee smirked, "but they here now, you feel me?"

"Fo' sho'. So what is it you think you know that I don't?"

"His baby mama," Vee said, telling a half truth. Karrin was definitely Ty's; she just wasn't baby mama.

Hardy nodded.

"So we just snatch her up torture the bitch—"

Vee cut him off by shaking his head.

"Naw, 'cause she don't know where he at, but believe me, he'll come for her," Vee surmised.

"How can you be so sure?"

"'Cause I am," Vee replied firmly, looking Hardy in the eyes.

"But you gotta be willin' to do what you ain't never

done."

"What's that?" Hardy wanted to know.

"Nothing," Vee smiled. "You gotta be willin' to sit on this bitch night and day and do absolutely nothing, and wait for Ty to come to you."

Vee was thinking of the night he fucked Karrin. The night they used each other's body to relieve their own guilt. He thought of her climax, the intensity of her embrace, the urgency of her need to feel his seed.

Vee knew then that she would break. That her love for him was stronger than her fear of any consequences he could represent. It was only a matter of time before she told Ty where she was. It was that emotion Vee was counting on, that emotion he would use Hardy to exploit.

Ty will come to you.

"I feel you, dawg. That shit make sense," Hardy agreed. "Yo," he added with a chuckle in his tone and madness in his eyes, "is she pretty?"

Vee knew why he was asking. He knew what Hardy intended to do.

"Who's baby is it?" he had asked.

"Kev," she had answered.

Kev's baby, your brother's baby.

Your brother was your enemy, the gangsta he was growled.

The baby is your blood, the demon within laughed.

It wasn't said to convince Vee to save the baby, but to taunt him with the fact he was forever cursed to shed his own blood.

Vee's temples flexed and his jaw line went rigid, but he knew what he had to do.

"Leave her out of that."

"For what?" Hardy bassed as if nobody was safe.

"Because we gonna use her to get Guy Simmons too," Vee said and cracked a half grin.

Hardy's expression went from defiant to understanding to one of admiration.

"Ay, yo, dawg, you a cold-blooded motherfucka!" Hardy laughed.

They shook hands on the deal, and Vee gave him Karrin's address.

"Night and day, yo, but trust me, you won't have long to wait," Vee assured him as he got in the car then chirped out.

The next day Tito and Vee met. Tito had a plane to catch. Vee agreed to drive him to the airport, but when Tito saw the Ferrari, he asked to drive. Vee tossed him the keys. Tito opened it up as they sped toward the airport.   "You know my first real car was a Ferrari," Tito reminisced, switching gears expertly. "First nigguh in Harlem with this shit. Back then nigguhs like Aldo, AZ, and Rich Porter, God bless the dead, set the trends. But when I came through wit' the drop-top magnum PT shit ... " Tito laughed.

Vee allowed a smile to creep across his face. He couldn't resist. He loved arrogance. He just didn't know why Tito wanted to talk to him, so he played his hand close to his chest.

"Dumbest shit I ever did," Tito said, shaking his head and dipping in and out of lanes effortlessly. "But we all learn from our mistakes, you know?"

"Fo' sho'," Vee replied.

Tito glanced over at Vee. He could see this young boy would be hard to crack. He switched the gears of the car and the conversation.

"So what was that all about between you and my cousin?" Tito inquired.

"Ask your cousin," Vee shot back.

I am, Tito chuckled to himself, but said, "I did. He told me to ask you. Let me tell you from jump, fam, I ain't trying to come at you sideways. Of course, under normal circumstances, I would definitely take my cousin's side, right or wrong. But me and Tre talked, and he told me you a solid dude. He fuck wit' you for real. That shit carry weight wit' me because he like a brother to me," Tito expressed.

But all Vee heard was that they discussed it.

Vee wasn't feeling that statement. Like Tre had to somehow hold Tito off of him. Tito read his tone.

"Not like that, fam. Tre ain't plead no pass for you. It was more like we brothers—Vee your man, Ty my man, so let them be men, see that? We stayin' neutral."

Vee didn't respond, so Tito continued.

"Make no mistake, Vee, if Tito Bell nod, I can bring the whole East. That type of weight can change a situation, but I'm not tryin' to throw that around."

Vee looked at him.

"So what's this? A warning about what you could do?"

Tito smiled.

"The type of cat I feel you are and the type of cat I'm known to be," Tito said, then looked at Vee, "we don't give warnings. I can see why Tre fuck wit' you. I like your style. It's gonna be good being partners."

Vee shot Tito a look.

"Partners?"

"Yeah. Red Light. Tre brought me in. What? You ain't know? My bad, fam," Tito said sincerely. He truly thought Vee knew.

Vee was heated. Not only had Tre and Tito been discussing his beef with Ty like they were Gods granting the mercy of restraint, but now Tre was treating the company like Vee was a peon, an employee!

"It was a power move, Vee, trust me. I can open a lot of doors, yo. Especially with y'all in negotiation with Charles Communications. I can handle Vanya, believe me."

Tito watched Vee for a reaction, but Vanya was the furthest thing from Vee's mind.

They arrived at the airport. Tito grabbed his suit bag and carry-on, and they both got out.

"How long you known Vanya?" Tito probed.

"I don't. I was just taking Tre's place at the meeting."

Satisfied, Tito nodded. He handed Vee the key. Tito extended his hand.

Vee shook it.

"Listen, Vee, I know shit is crazy, but I ain't your enemy. I know from where you stand and where you think I stand, it might seem miles apart. But life is like a mirror for two reasons. One, to reflect upon. And two, because things in it may be closer than they appear," Tito said, then smiled and started to go away. He stopped and turned back. "Oh, yeah, Tre said you wanted to pour me a drink. What about?"

Vee stood by the car. As he opened the door and

slid behind the wheel, he replied, "Let him tell you."

Tito's brow curled for a moment, then he shrugged and turned away.

Vee drove off, checking his rearview mirror, watching everything in it get farther and farther away.

●●●●●●

Gloria's one-day excursion had turned into three days.

She and Guy never left the room and wore no more than a smile and each other's scent the whole time. No matter what was going on or how old she got, nobody did it like Guy. He ran her from any other man, in more ways than one. Besides, for Gloria, an orgasm with Guy was like Lay's chips—you can't have just one.

At the airport, Gloria kissed Guy on the cheek.

"I'll call you when I reach New York," she said.

"You know you don't have to do this, Glo," Guy replied, slipping his arm around her waist.

Gloria slipped out of his embrace and sighed longingly.

"I wish I didn't, baby. But you too old to change, and I'm too old to keep putting up with it. Let's try it like this for a while, okay?"

"Hit and run?" he quipped.

"Gotta be number one," Gloria said, using the hook of the old song "Hit and Run" to answer him.

They both laughed.

"The Flash Inn," Guy chuckled. "We used to dance all night."

"I used to dance all night. Them big-ass feet of yours used to sit you down," she snickered.

"That was an excuse. I just wanted to watch you move," Guy replied sincerely. "I love you, Glo Bell."

"I love you too, country boy."

The moment passed. Then the flight was announced and reality set in.

"Don't forget what we talked about," Gloria reminded him. "Do the right thing for a change, baby. Okay?"

Guy grinned.

"When haven't I?"

Gloria gathered up her travel bag. She started to walk away. Stopped. Turned back.

"Guy?"

"Yeah?"

"Who is she?"

He didn't respond.

"You hate to be alone, so I know you not."

Guy looked at her, knowing she at least deserved the truth.

"Shantelle."

"Oh." Gloria nodded like she had received a subtle blow. "At least you kept it in the family, huh? Good-bye, Guy."

Guy watched her strut away, regretting all the pain he had ever caused her, but knowing there was nothing he could do about it. He checked his watch and headed to the private plane he had chartered for his own flight.

The whole flight back to New York Gloria thought about the bind her life was becoming. For years she had poured herself into being a wife, only to have Guy so nonchalantly pull that rug from under her. Then she made her purpose of being Kev. Now he was gone and she felt empty. She had come to New York for a new start and found herself faced with old demons, namely her complacency in relation to Eddie's death. Now she stood on the very brink.

You gonna kill him yourself.

Asia's words chilled her to the bone. Gloria was feisty, a fighter, and a survivor, but she was no killer. Especially when it came to Guy. His smile melted her anger, leaving her naked to her most vulnerable emotions. If she couldn't even stay mad at him, how could she kill him?

Then you die. The choice is yours.

Her own life hung in the balance. She thought again of the one person she knew could help. The closer the moment came, the more she believed it was her only chance.

She sailed through Manhattan traffic in a cab driven by a flirtatious African brother. She put him on mute. When she got to Theresa's brownstone, all she wanted was a nice bath and a glass of wine. What she got was ...

"Hello, Gloria."

She spun around, knowing her mind had to be playing tricks on her. It wasn't. It was Guy, leaning against the trunk of a Lincoln from a car service. The driver sat inside, waiting patiently.

"Guy?! What are you ... why are —" she stammered, not realizing the meaning of his presence.

"Surprise, baby," he smiled, approaching and returning her kiss on the cheek from the airport. "You happy to see me, right?"

Gaining her composure, Gloria asked, "Guy, what are you up to?"

"I could ask you the same thing." He smiled, but his eyes didn't. "Come on, let's go inside."

They walked up the steps together. Gloria unlocked the door and they went in. Inside, Theresa was watching "The Real Housewives of Atlanta" and eating her favorite combination: chocolate-covered cherries and champagne.

"Glo, come look at what this trifling bitch Nene got on," she remarked, then looked up and saw Guy. Her whole face brightened up. "Heeey, brah-in-law. What a surprise."

She got up and gave Guy a big hug. Gloria internally cringed at the greeting Theresa gave Guy. She felt low allowing Theresa to think she was embracing family when she was really embracing her husband's killer.

"I knew it, Glo. I knew this nigguh couldn't stay away from you, girl! You musta really put it on him this time," Theresa laughed.

Guy laughed. Gloria didn't.

"Yeah, my baby definitely got her hooks in me, but, uh, I needed to handle some business in Connecticut, so I decided to stop by," Guy lied.

"Well, sit down, relax. I haven't cooked, but you welcomed to anything but my chocolate-covered cherries," Theresa giggled. "I'm sorry the girls aren't here."

Guy and Gloria sat side by side. Guy placed his hand on Gloria's crossed thigh.

"I know how these young people is, busy, busy, busy. Especially Tito. Matter of fact, where is Tito? I needed to speak to him," Guy said, coming to the real reason he was in New York. He turned to Gloria, "Why don't you call ol' Tito. Let's go see him! But don't tell him I'm here. Let's surprise him," Guy winked, and it hit Gloria why Guy was there.

Guy knew Gloria had told Tito about him killing Eddie. He didn't need to ask. He knew Gloria well enough to see it in her. He also knew it was Tito who put her up to lobbying for Ty. So he had come to confront Tito on his terms. Unannounced. Without warning. Just like he did that night at Eddie's.

"Call him," he repeated, and Gloria saw the same look as the night of Nicky Barnes' party, when he was choking her in the bathroom. This wasn't the Guy she loved or the Guy she hated, it was the Guy she feared.

She called Tito.

Tito had just gotten back from Miami. Brooklyn had picked him up from the airport.

"Yo," he answered.

"Hey, nephew," Gloria greeted, trying to sound cheery and keep the quiver out of her tone.

"What's going on?" he replied.

"I'm back."

In those two words, he heard it all. "I'm back" meant we need to talk, and the quiver told him shit wasn't all good.

"Where you at?"

"At your mama's."

"I'm on my way," Tito replied, then hung up. "Go to mommy house."

"Why? What's up?" Brooklyn asked, laying on her horn and giving the driver in front of her the finger.

"Gloria back."

Brooklyn sucked her teeth.

"You and Asia soft as fuck."

Tito didn't respond. Then it occurred to him the twins were inseparable. "Where is Asia anyway?"

Brooklyn regretted mentioning her name. She shrugged her shoulders, but she was too brutally honest to be a good liar.

"Fuck you mean—" Tito said, then shrugged his shoulders, mocking her. "Where she at?"

"Philly."

"For what?"

"I don't know."

"You fuckin' lyin'. You do know," Tito snapped, tired of her bullshit.

"I said I don't fuckin' know!" she barked, but there was no bite to it.

He studied her profile for a minute, then called Asia. She picked up on the third ring.

"How was Mi—" she began, but he cut her off.

"Where you at?"

"Queens."

He hung up in her face. He speed-dialed another number.

"Peace, brah. How you," Nazir greeted.

"Peace, fam. Put Asia on the phone," Tito said.

He could hear Nazir chuckle as he handed Asia the phone. She didn't say anything, but Tito could hear her presence.

"I'ma beat yo ass," was all he said, then hung up. He looked at Brooklyn and added, "Yours too."

Brooklyn finally broke her silence when they got to the brownstone.

"I told her she stupid. Fuck you goin' for? The nigguh got a whole wife! But you know how Asia do. As soon as—"

"Brooklyn."

"Huh?"

"Shut up."

Tito noticed the car service and the waiting driver. They ascended the stairs and rang the bell. Theresa answered and kissed them both. When they walked in, they both froze.

"Hello, Tito," Guy greeted, rising confidently from the couch.

Tito looked from Guy to Gloria. Her gaze seemed to say, It's not my fault.

"I told your aunt I wanted to surprise you," Guy said, extending his hand.

Tito hesitated then shook it.

"Pleasantly surprised, Unk," Tito replied.

"Hello, Brooklyn. Or are you Asia," Guy joked, then kissed her on the cheek. It was like kissing stone. Guy knew why.

"What's up, Guy?" she retorted, making a point not to say uncle.

She shot Gloria daggers. She blamed it on Gloria's treachery. Tito knew better. He had simply underestimated the elder gangsta. He could've walked into a setup. That was Guy's point, to let him know that. Tito wouldn't make that mistake again.

"Come, nephew, I'm due in Connecticut. Let's you and I have a drink on the back patio."

It was a bricked-in enclosure that Theresa had brought to life with a flower garden patio set and mahogany bar. Tito poured them both a drink, then handed Guy his.

"Theresa better not let anybody find out she got a bar on the back patio. You'll have every wino in Harlem trying to sale the walk," Guy chuckled.

"So what brings you to my city, Unk?" Tito questioned. "Well, you know, I'ma ol' country boy at heart. I love my fish and grits, but Harlem … Harlem's my kind of town. Lot of memories here, lots of regrets," Guy answered, then sipped his drink.

"Regrets?" Tito echoed.

Guy sat at the patio table and motioned for Tito to join him.

"Of course. Who don't? I mean, if you ain't got no regrets, it mean you never really lived, you know? Never made bad decisions that seemed good at the time. Without mistakes, there are no lessons."

Tito nodded and drank to the jewel. It seemed like Guy was apologizing for what Tito would never accept.

"But some bad decisions you can't come back from. Sometimes your whole life becomes a mistake," Tito threw back.

Guy cupped his glass with both hands. "That's true. But how do we know? How do you know when you're livin' a mistake, or better yet, when living is a mistake?"

Guy smiled. There was no mistaking the real conversation they were having. He replied without a smile. "When the lights go out?"

Guy laughed heartily.

"I like that. When the lights go out?" he repeated. He got up, grabbed the liquor bottle, and brought it back to the table. He refreshed Tito's drink, then sat, and poured himself another finger.

"But, hey, one thing you should never dwell on is a regret or a mistake. What's done is done. What can you do about it?" Guy asked with a hint of challenge in his tone.

Tito tensed but didn't let it show.

"Life is about movin' on, getting past the past," Guy said, then raised his glass. "To new beginnings."

Tito toasted.

"To new beginnings."

Guy downed the drink in one shot.

Now, that'll put hair on your chest. Like this thing with you and me. The Bells and the Simmonses. The force you bring, the resources … you have power. And I understand because I bring the same, maybe a little more … slightly," Guy winked. "With that kind of power, together … unstoppable. Unless that power was to crash. Then it would be tragic."

Tito heard the innuendo in Guy's words and didn't flinch to meet it.

"Why would they crash?"

"Mistakes," Guy shot back. "I'm talking about Ty."

"Ty?" Tito echoed.

Guy sat back, playing his hand like an expert.

"Ty's young, hotheaded. He's still got a lot to learn. And me? I got a few mo' miles left in me, so just for the time being, you deal directly with me on this deal. Not Ty."

They both smiled, but for different reasons. Guy

knew Ty was sharp, but he was sharper. Guy's smile was saying, Now try that junk you pulled with Gloria and Ty on me. Tito's smile said, I welcome the challenge.

"Does Ty know?"

"He will," Guy replied, standing up. "Like I said, I don't know. Maybe Ty isn't the man to run this family after me. Maybe you are."

And that was Guy's weak card. Aces don't only win hands. Sometimes it's whose lowest card is higher.

Tito sat back and took it in.

"I'm not a Simmons," Tito remarked.

Neither is Ty, Guy thought bitterly, but said, "The Bells and the Simmonses should be one. Without Eddie, where would I be? Anyway, just something to think about, you know?"

Guy walked out, leaving Tito doing just that: thinking. Tito saw the carrot on the stick. But he also saw something even more subtle: Guy's suggestion had made Ty and Tito potential competitors. Why back Ty when Tito could back himself? Tito smiled to himself, then raised his glass.

"You're good, Unk. Goddamn good. But I will win."

With that, Tito downed his whole drink in one shot.

CHAPTER 45

Four Months Earlier

The investigation had been a success.

The investigation had been a failure.

The investigation had been a success because a suspect had been arrested and charged. David "Lil' Man" Baker, 17, was the suspect. His fingerprints were all over the crime scene, near the victims, on the victims. He was caught red-handed.

The media had played on plastering his face all over the front page and six o'clock news. The DA was seeking the death penalty. The mayor was seeking re-election. Detective Sergeant Randall was seeking lieutenant bars. They all were expecting Franklin to congratulate and possibly promote him, but Franklin was seeking only the truth.

"Hey, Frank, let it go, okay? If the kid wants to try for this alone, what can you do? The justice is someone will be held accountable for the heinous crime," Randall had tried to convince him.

To which Franklin replied, "The justice hasn't been served. It's only been appeased."

That was why the investigation had been a failure. Lil' Man wasn't talking. He refused all attempts to implicate anyone to the crime. The most they got off of him was, "I don't know shit about no Wolf Pack, and I don't know shit about no Boo, but I do know I'm tired of looking at your fuckin' face."

Boo, the leader of the young Wolf Pack, couldn't be found, but his presence was felt and the impact drove Franklin closer to his temptation. Young Darnell simply wanted to be down and hanging out with the young Wolf Pack made him important in his own eyes. He was accepted amongst the only somebodys in a hood full of nobodys.

Franklin's raid changed it all.

When the raid jumped off, Boo handed the gun to Darnell.

"Lil' D, take this shit and bounce!"

And he did. Right into the arms of the law. Franklin was sick. He browbeat him, chastised him, and then he did the worst thing he could've done: He got Darnell off.

"Look, Randall, I know the boy. He's a good kid. He just made a bad decision. Let me just take him home to his mother," Franklin said.

Randall said okay. Franklin took him home. Somebody saw Franklin bring Darnell home. That somebody told somebody else who told somebody who told Boo.

Darnell went to the same church as the detective. Darnell had been at the house. Darnell knew Lil' Man and Boo ran the young Wolf Pack. Darnell got caught with a gun but came home the same night, courtesy of the detective.

"Who else knew?" somebody had asked Boo. Nobody knew it was Silk the whole time. Boo was looking for Darnell, and when he found him ...

⬤⬤⬤⬤⬤⬤

Franklin rushed to the hospital as fast as he could. He

even used his siren to get him through red lights. The reverend had called him as soon as he heard.

By the time he got to the hospital, the doctor was coming out to talk to the reverend and Ms. Jenkins.

"How ... how," Ms. Jenkins stammered through tears.

"How is he, doctor?" the reverend asked for her.

"Your son's going to be fine, Ms. Jenkins," the doctor announced happily.

"Oh, thank you, Jesus," Ms. Jenkins exclaimed as if she had been hit with the spirit.

"He's a strong boy. The bullet hit no major arteries. It went right through the base of the throat. He may have some difficulty speaking for a while, but it should clear up. Other than that, his broken ribs and jaw will heal."

"Thank you, doctor," the reverend said, shaking his hand. The doctor walked away.

Franklin opened his arms to Ms. Jenkins.

"Ms. Jenkins, I'm so – "

She pushed him away violently, shocking and confusing Franklin.

"Get away from me! Stay away from me! Stay away from my son!" she shrieked with all her pent-up fear and frustration. People turned in their direction.

"Now, Sister Jenkins, please calm – "

"No!" she barked defiantly. "It is his fault this happened to Darnell!"

"My fault?" Franklin repeated, aghast.

"Darnell is a good boy! A good boy! You had no right to use his goodness for your own ends!" she accused.

"Ms. Jenkins, I have never used Darnell in any way," Franklin replied firmly.

"They thought he was talking to you. That's why they did it! They said he told you about them boys and what they did!

How could you involve my baby in such foolishness?" she ranted madly.

Franklin's heart fell to his stomach. Use Darnell? Darnell talking?

"Darnell never told me anything!"

"When will you learn, detective, your justice just don't work for us? We ain't got guns and badges to protect us! Those boys saw Darnell and they beat him with a bat! Then they shot him and ... and doused him with gas," she said, her voice trailing off.

Franklin plopped down in a vacant seat, thinking this could not be happening. All he tried to do was help Darnell and it had almost cost him his life.

Why? Which is always the first question towards despair.

When she gained her composure, Ms. Jenkins told him firmly, "Stay away from Darnell. He won't be coming to any of your classes, and he won't be going on any trips. Just stay away!"

She went to see Darnell, with the reverend supporting her.

The first thing Franklin did was withdraw from teaching the classes in the church. The people shunned him. The neighborhood looked the other way when he came around. He began to rely on Silk's information more and more. It was Silk who pulled his coat to what happened to the baller, his baby mother, and the little girl.

"Whoever he is, he want Ty Simmons bad," Silk had told him.

When Franklin investigated, he found it to be true. Several such murder-robbery-rapes had occurred in Goldsboro, Smithfield, Raleigh, Greensboro, and now Durham. What really caught Franklin's attention was every victim had some connection to Ty Simmons or the Wolf Pack. That couldn't have been a coincidence.

Finally the investigation breathed life. He threw himself into it. It was the only thing that kept him from going crazy. Doing the right thing has to count for something, he thought.

He had received no affirmation. But he did receive a phone call from Silk. Franklin had checked his voicemail and heard:

"Yo, Franklin, this your man Silk! Boy, have I got news for you!"

The first time Tito had ever seen Vito Sarducci was at his father's funeral. He stuck out because he and his three henchmen were the only white faces in attendance. He had approached Theresa after the funeral. Vito said something in Italian, crossed himself in Catholic fashion, then said, "Your husband was a man of honor and he will be missed. If there is anything you need, anything at all, I will be insulted if you ask of anyone but of Vito Sarducci." He said something else in Italian, crossed himself again, then left the cemetery. From then on, it was Vito who supplied Theresa with protection for her numbers racket and coke for her side hustle. It was Vito who had been the family's silent godfather.

Tito remembered the feeling he felt. It was a wordless admiration until he learned the word for it. The word was respect. That was the feeling he felt when he walked into the little brick house out in the Bronx. Vinnie walked him into the living room, then left back out. The whole house smelled of Italian sausage and onions. Tito could see Vito through the partition that led to the kitchen. Tony Bennett played in the background.

"Come a little closer, will ya, kid? I don't see too good," Vito called from the kitchen.

Tito entered the kitchen. Vito wiped his hands on a dishrag and asked, "You know who I am?"

"Yeah, Mr. Sarducci," Tito replied.

Vito shook Tito's hand, then his stern scowl broke into a smile.

"Look at youse … little Tito all grown up," he chuckled. "Looking like your father, may he rest in peace. Sit down. Let's talk. Eat. You can tell me if I use too many onions. My wife, she always says that."

"Thanks, Mr. Sarducci, but I don't eat pork," Tito responded.

Vito stopped stirring the sauce and scowled slightly.

"Don't eat pork? Who doesn't eat pork? Who are you, Malcolm freakin' X? Listen, Tito, number one, never say you don't eat something to a guy tryin' to break bread with youse. You know why?"

"Why?"

"Because what he hears is you don't eat his_somethin', you follow me? Instead, you say you're not hungry or you just ate. Then he says eat. So you talk, you pick at the food, you talk some more, you drink the wine. The guy asks wassa matta, why you're not eatin'? Then you say you don't eat pork. Now he goes, 'Christ! Why didn't you tell me?!' He makes a fuss, but he's satisfied, you're satisfied, and now you're ready to do business, capece?" Vito schooled him.

Tito chuckled. "I got you, Mr. Sarducci."

"Okay," Vito smiled, then set a big plate of pasta and pork in front of Tito and sat down in front of his own plate. "It's all bullshit, but this is how business is done."

"I guess I should thank you for what you did for me tonight. But believe me, it was all under control," Tito remarked with the bravado of youth.

Mr. Sarducci smiled as he ate his pasta.

"Christl! This is fuckin' delicious! What is she talkin' about, too many onions?" Vito said then wiped his mouth.

"When your mother told me she kicked you out, I told her good for her. I've been tellin' her for years that she's spoilin' you rotten, but you know women," Vito waved it off dismissively and sipped his wine. "You know I met your father thought Joey Gallo. Crazy Joe Gallo. Your father was a man of respect. He was one of the best guys I ever knew."

Vito lifted up his glass and Tito met his toast. They both drank to Eddie.

"Whoever killed him was the scum of the earth," Vito said with disgust. He looked Tito in the eyes and said, "And listen to what I tell you: Whoever killed him, it was someone he knew. Mark my words. A man like your father don't die in his own living room in his robe and not know who done it. Remember that."

Tito nodded.

"My mother said the same thing. She always thought Nicky Barnes had something to do with it."

"Fuck Nicky Barnes. We made that gumbah and he turns rat. May he rot and die slow. But it wasn't him. Who benefitted? Answer that and you'll have the scum," Vito jeweled him, then bit his sausage. "I know you coulda handled that thing tonight, but hey, everybody needs a friend, right?"

Tito smirked.

"Indeed."

Vito looked at Tito's plate.

"You haven't touched your food."

"I don't eat pork."

"Christ! Why didn't you tell me?!" Vito laughed, making his earlier point. "Maybe you'll like dessert better."

Vito got up and took Tito's plate. Tito's beeper went off. He checked it. When he looked up, Vito had another plate in front of him. On it was a white brick-sized package wrapped in plastic. It was a kilo of cocaine. Tito looked up at Vito's smiling face.

"What can I tell ya, I'm all outta ice cream," he winked. "Can you handle this?"

"Hell yeah!" Tito replied with gusto.

Vito sat down.

"I'm givin' you this chance out of love for your father. My debt to him is now paid. If you should prove unworthy, no hard feelings, but all bets are off. But if you should truly prove to be your father's son, then you will be a very rich man, capece?" he asked.

"Capece," Tito confirmed.

And so it began. Fast forward one month. Tre converts his weed gates to crack gates and keeps them open around the clock. Sleep goes back home to Brooklyn and sets up shop in Brownsville. Tito does the same in Harlem and the Lower East Side.

Fast forward six months.

The Dreads retaliate and murder some of Tito's workers in Spanish Harlem, but times have changed. Tito is heavy in three boroughs, and in three boroughs Dreads start dropping like raindrops. Tito and Black Rose reach a truce and become each other's best customers. Tito pushes all the weed off on his man in Newark and Jersey City. By the end of one month, Tito counts $500,000.

Fast Forward One Year

Tito is the first nigguh in Harlem with a Ferrari. They call it Magnum P.I. after the TV show because it's a red convertible. He pulls up at the Rucker with a bad

Puerto Rican mami form Brooklyn who had just done a flick with Spike Lee. He loved her sexy accent.

"Yo, get the fuck outta here, nigguh!" Sleep exclaimed in his usual laid-back style.

Sleep was with his man Calvin Klein and Sean from Marcy in Sleep's money-green Acura Legend with the Batman kit and hammers. He gave Tito a gangsta hug.

"Yo, Po! Alpo! What up, nigguh?! You got next or what?!" Tito shouted at his man Alpo, another Harlem legend known for stuntin' and flossin'.

Alpo gave a smile and the finger, jumped on his blue and white ninja motorcycle and barked out. Ten minutes later, Alpo came back with a black Saab convertible, parked it, and jogged around the corner. A moment later he pulled up in a Silver Volvo 740 with the drop kit, parked it, and ran around the corner.

"Stop, Po! You killlin' 'em. Oh, my God, you killin' 'em!" someone in the crowd yelled and mad laughter ensued.

A minute later, Alpo pulled up in a candy-apple red Corvette with gold BBS and stood on the hood like, WHAT! He hed his arms out like Jesus.

"Fuck that! Fuck that! It took three for my one, nigguh! You shoulda did it right the first time!" Tito chuckled.

Alpo came off the hood and gave Tito love.

"Tito, Tito, Tito!" Rosie chimed in her sexy Brooklyn accent, holding up her car phone.

He came over and took the phone. "Fuck you doin' answerin' it anyway?"

"It was ringin'," she shrugged.

"Yo," Tito answered.

"Vito wanna see you." He hung up the phone and looked at Sleep.

"Ay, yo, Sleep, take Rosie home for me."

"Just 'cause I answered the phone, Mookie?" she quizzed.

"Naw, love, I just gotta handle something. Beep me," Tito replied getting in the car.

Rosie got out and sat in the backseat of Sleep's Acura with Sean.

"Bye, Mookie!" she called out as Tito sped off.

Vito was down on the Lower East Side of Manhattan at a sports club he owned. He and two other older Italians were playing cards outside at a small table while his bodyguard/driver stood vigilant.

Tito pulled up and got out. He approached the table.

"What's goin' on, Unk," Tito questioned.

Vito didn't respond. Instead, he finished his hand, taking his time. Tito knew when he was upset about something, so he waited. When the hand was over, the two Italians went inside.

"You too," Vito told his bodyguard.

When they were alone, Vito turned to Tito and asked casually, "Tell me, Tito, do you know what a nigga is?"

Tito tensed visibly. Any other white man would've been picking themselves off the ground, but Tito knew Vito was far from prejudice.

Vito saw Tito tense up. "Maybe you don't hear so good, eh? I asked you, do you know what a nig—"

"I know what it is," Tito seethed.

"Do you?" Vito smirked as he sat back in his chair. "What is it?"

"You tell me."

"Oh, now you want me to tell you."

"Yeah, tell me!"

Vito leaned his elbows on the table and replied, "A nigga is a man that has found a way to defy the laws of physics and has learned how to keep his foot in his own goddamn neck!" Vito stayed calm until he got to the last emphasized word and slammed his fist on the table for punctuation. "What the hell is that?" he spat, gesturing wildly to the car. "A hundred-thousand-dollar police magnet, red as a fuckin' target and driven by an 18-year-old, unemployed black kid from Harlem! You tell me what's wrong wit' that picture, then close your eyes and tell me that ain't a nigga you see drivin' that car!"

"I ain't no nigga, man," Tito growled. Uncle figure or no uncle figure, Vito was pushing it.

"I know you don't like that word, but you don't beat it by gettin' mad, you beat it by bein' smart," Vito said as he pointed to his own head. "I'm sixty-friggin'-eight years old and I never seen the inside of a cell. You know why? 'Cause I don't ride around with a fuckin' 'arrest me' sign pinned to my ass!" Vito fumed.

Tito couldn't say anything because he knew Vito was right.

"Would you rather have a thousand bucks in your pocket or look like you have a thousand bucks in your pocket?" Vito quipped.

Tito didn't answer, but Vito saw what he wanted to say in his eyes.

"And that's your problem right there," Vito retorted, then picked up the cards and began shuffling. "Now get outta here. And leave the keys on the table."

Tito just looked at Vito, but Vito dealt out a hand of Solitaire.

"Goddamn, Unk, a hundred grand?"

Vito looked up and shrugged, "What a waste."

Tito slammed the keys on the table and left, vexed. It was a hundred - thousand-dollar hundred-dollar lesson that kept him from making a million-dollar mistake. The next summer, the Feds hit Harlem hard, but Tito was too far below the radar to register a blip.

●●●●●●

Tito sat on the couch, flipping through channels randomly. He saw Charles Communications ad several times and smiled to himself. He checked his watch: 5:37 a.m. The rising sun over Harlem confirmed it. He was in Asia and Brooklyn's brownstone in Sugar Hill. Brooklyn had long ago went to bed. He was wide awake. Waiting. Asia walked in singing Floetry's "It's Getting Late" until she saw Tito. She wanted to be upset because she was grown, but instead, she smiled and said, "I'm not seventeen no more, Tito."

"Thank God," he chuckled lightly. Then the smile faded as he added, "Guy offered me the Simmons family."

Asia sat down on the couch next to him.

"Wow. Just like that?"

Tito shook his head.

"It was more indirect. Unstated, you know? The way somebody just throws words at you, but you can see it still carried weight," he explained.

"Like a carrot on a stick."

"Exactly."

"You think he's serious?"

"Maybe. One thing I do know is he know we know about Daddy," he informed her.

"Should we ..." she began, letting innuendo finish her sentence.

"Naw. That wasn't the vibe I got. I'm thinking maybe he feel like even if we don't get him, that we'll get at Ty after he go. So it's like, here, take the keys as long as you don't push Ty out the car later, feel me?" Tito surmised.

Asia nodded. "Makes sense."

"Does it?" he smirked. "I killed your father for the mother lode, so here's the mother lode so you don't have to kill my son," Tito shook his head. "But we 'posed to be family. At some point, that's gotta count for something', don't it?"

"With us it do."

Tito wiped his face as if to reset his mental. He looked at Asia solemnly.

"I know you not seventeen, Asia. But I see you. It's written all over your face. Don't get me wrong, Nazir is a solid motherfucka, but it's a bad decision for two reasons: He is in the game and he married."

Asia kicked off her shoes, tucked her legs under, and replied, "Don't you think I've thought about that? I mean, like, him being in the game ain't really an issue because it ain't like I got a nine-to-five myself, you know? But the married part ..."

Tito cut in on her pause. "He ain't leavin' her."

"I know."

"And you good with being the side chick?" he asked

skeptically. "The me-me-me girl is Gucci with being Ms. Booty Call?"

"Hell no," she retorted defensively, "but I'm peace with equal status."

"A second wife?"

She nodded, eyeing his reaction.

"Wow," he expressed. "I mean, I'm a man, so I can dig havin' a harem, but you my sister and I know you."

"I respect Nazir. He hasn't tried to touch me. If I'm not his wife, he won't have sex with me. What dude you know, married or not, besides you or a faggot, gonna pass this up?" she asked arrogantly.

"Well, besides objecting to being in the same category as a cocksucker, I feel you," Tito replied.

Asia mushed him and laughed.

"You know what I mean, niggah. He respects me and he is worthy of my respect. He solid and, Lord, he so preeetyyy," she giggled.

"Do you love him?" Tito asked, looking in her eyes.

"I never been in love, but I never felt like this neither," she responded sincerely.

Tito shrugged.

"I guess that deads the Scarface shit. I can't tell him to stay away from my sister 'cause my sister ain't gonna stay away from him. I just hope you know what you doin'."

"Me too," she admitted.

Tito studied her face, seeing all the years, all the memories, and all the reasons she was precious to him.

"Sometimes I regret when we were sixteen after that … thing you told us—the only flag we rep is our last name?"

Tito grimaced at the memory, but grinned at his words.

"I remember."

"Then I guess we was born into this."

"I guess so," he agreed, then he stood. "Go to bed lil' girl."

"Yes, Papa Dumbbell," she answered, using the name the twins called him when they were little.

He laughed as he walked out the door.

⚫⚫⚫⚫⚫⚫⚫

Ty stood at The Corner Pub in Greensboro, kicking it with a white girl who looked like Kim Kardashian. They were watching a UNC- Georgetown game when a young black dude walked up to them and smiled at Ty without saying anything. Ty looked him up and down and knew right away he was a cop.

"Can I help you, officer?" Ty quipped, sipping his beer.

"How you know I'm a cop?" he shot back.

"You smell like one, just like bacon sizzling," Ty joked and the girl laughed.

"Actually, that was the double-bacon cheeseburger that — never mind. But you are right about the cop part," he said, then flashed his detective shield and ID. "Detective Franklin, Durham P.D."

"Durham? This is Greensboro. You lost or somethin'?"

"Naw, it's just that I heard you'd be here tonight, and I thought I'd come by and meet the infamous Tyquan Simmons," Franklin replied.

Ty whispered in the girl's ear. She left. Franklin took her place.

"How word in Greensboro reach all the way in Durham?" Ty wanted to know.

Franklin shrugged. "Hood Twitter," he retorted sarcastically.

"You're a hood snitch!" Ty spat with a sneer.

"Does it matter? It's not like you're hiding, right? This guy who's stalking you knows where you are because you wanted him to, from the looks of things. You look ready for war," Franklin remarked, surveying the room.

He was right. Ty had his team of six dudes and four chicks scattered throughout the room. To the naked eye, they were just faces in the crowd. But Franklin peeped how they were strategically placed and how all of them were watching him and Ty.

"I bet it's enough firepower in here to give out Fed numbers," Franklin.

He had definitely caught Ty slipping because Ty had two 4-calibers, one made fully automatic, on him. But he didn't let it show. He mockingly extended his hands, wrists together.

"So arrest me."

Franklin waved him off, looked at the TV.

"I'm more interested in the Wolf Pack than possession of a firearm by a felon," Franklin said.

"Well, as you can see, I'm a Tar Heel fan myself," Ty replied.

"Naw, Ty, the real Wolf Pack. Your Wolf Pack," Franklin grinned, moving in for the kill.

"I don't know what you're talking about," Ty answered, downing his beer.

"Well, let me put it like this," Franklin said, then pulled up the pics on his phone and held it up for him to see it. Ty looked at the first one, the body of Banks' grandmother, then continued to look at the screen.

"These are the four reasons I get up in the morning. These are the four thoughts I have right before I go to bed, and these are the four reasons I came all the way to Greensboro. I got the names. Yours and Vee's. One of you ordered this and one of you will burn for this, I guarantee. Now, the only question is who," Franklin explained.

Ty knew that Banks' whole family had been murdered. He knew it had been the Wolf Pack and that a lot of people in the street thought he ran the Wolf Pack. Find that person and he would find the snitch.

"I guess this is the part where you offer me a deal and I tell you to suck my dick, right? Or have we reached that yet?" Ty smirked, letting Franklin know the conversation was over.

Franklin nodded, ignoring the insult.

"I guess we have, and if we're reading from the script, then my line is, 'I'm gonna get you, Simmons.' Well, that is, if this maniac you're running from doesn't get you first," Franklin tossed at him as he walked off.

Who was the snitch?

That was the question on Ty's mind as he drove to the motel with the white girl jabbering away drunkenly in the passenger's seat. He didn't hear a word she said. He was too busy trying to figure out who in Durham could've put them people on to him. Whoever did it was really trying to burn him because four bodies like that would get him the death penalty for sure. Before he'd let that happen, he'd murder his whole team in Durham himself just to make sure he didn't miss the snitch.

Ty's thoughts turned to Hardy. Hardy had been going hard, murdering Ty's people in all his spots. Then he just stopped. Ty's ego wanted to believe ever since he had been putting the word out where he'd be, Hardy had fallen back, but his gut told him otherwise. Ty didn't like the silence. He liked the loud approach. You could see that coming. Silence made him more edgy because you can't stop what you can't see.

When they got in the motel room, Ty was semi-conscious of the white girl's presence.

"I'm just gonna take a shower," she began to say as Ty snatched her to him and slid his hand under her skirt.

"Oh!" she exclaimed, surprised by his forcefulness but turned on just the same.

"Fuck a shower," he grumbled lustfully, pulling her skirt up and pinning her against the wall.

The girl represented nothing, a body, a nut rag on which to take out his frustration. He wasn't seeing her, he was seeing Karrin. Of all the problems on his plate, Karrin's absence was by far the biggest. Not only because she carried the secret that, once exposed, could ruin his chances of taking over the family and maybe even cost him his life, her absence bothered him because he loved her and hated to think that she was really gone.

Ty pushed aside her panties and penetrated the white girl four fingers deep. She gasped and clawed but the pain melted into a violently intense pleasure and made her moan in ecstasy.

She cocked her left leg up on his waist and grinded back.

"Oh, yes, babbby, yes!" she squealed.

He snatched up her shirt and bra in one motion and her large, firm breasts bounced free and loose. He wrapped his lips around the hard pink nipple and sucked until she grabbed the back of his head. The sensation made her cum all over his hand. She took his hand and put it in her mouth, feasting on her own juices while she loosened his belt and gripped his hard black dick. Ty snatched her off her feet. She wrapped her legs around his back, as he plunged deep into her tight pink pussy. He banged that pussy like he hated her, bouncing her on the full length of his shaft while she gasped and squealed.

"Oh ... my ... God! Oohhh ... Gooooddd," she bounced, holding on for dear life.

"Shut the fuck up," he hissed, sliding two fingers in her ass, making her cum instantly.

Feeling that familiar quiver in his stomach, Ty put her down and pushed her to her knees. He slapped her lips with his dick and slid it in and out her mouth until he was ready to cum. When he unloaded his seed all over her face and mouth, she didn't hesitate to devour what her tongue could reach.

"Mmmm," she moaned, eyeing him with lustful greed.

"Now you take a shower," Ty ordered her dismissively.

She did as she was told. The act only released pressure but brought no relief. His frustration still remained. He picked up the phone and dialed Karrin's number. He decided it was time to tell her what he had been holding back. The thing he didn't want her to know because of the doors it could open. Ty decided it was now or never.

He didn't know for sure, but his gut was telling him he was right. It had to be. It was why she wouldn't tell him where she was, but felt safe enough that he wouldn't find out. It had to be. It made sense. Cat was her cousin and Vee was Cat's man. If he was wrong, he risked exposing his hand, but he had to try. It had to be.

The phone went to voicemail like it had been doing, but this time he left a message.

"Baby, listen, I know you're scared. But you need to talk to me. I think I know where you're at, and if you're there, then you definitely ain't safe. You wit' Vee. If you are, and you told him anything, just know Vee is Guy's son too. He is not who you think he is, baby. Just please call me. I love you."

Ty hung up. There was nothing he could do now but wait. But he didn't have to wait long.

The phone rang. Karrin's picture flashed across the screen. He answered.

"Okay," she said.

CHAPTER 46

Rucker Park was packed. The famous basketball tournament was heating up, and Tito's team was in strong contention. But he wasn't watching the game. He and Tre were standing by Tre's car and Tre had just dropped the bomb.

"Yo, fam, you absolutely sure?" Tito stressed.

"My peoples ain't never missed, my niggauh. I'm one-hunnid," Tre replied firmly.

Tito shook his head.

"Goddamn,," he said, almost to himself.

Guy was a Federal informant. Tito couldn't believe his ears, but he knew Tre's connect always came through for them. This information changed everything. As much as he hated it, Tito knew he had to dead the plan to merge with the Simmonses. He had to dead any idea of expanding down South. There was no way he was doing business with an informant. On top of that, Guy knew about the Sarducci hit. No question, Tito thought, Guy has to go now. He thought about Ty. Did he know his father was a snitch? How could he not? Whether he knew or not, Tito couldn't take the chance. From that moment on, Guy and Ty ceased to keep breathing in Tito's mind. The rest was just a matter of pressing the button.

"What a waste," Tito mumbled, thinking of all the millions he'd never make because of abandoning the deal.

"My man Vee was supposed to tell you down Miami. But I haven't heard from him since. The young nigguh on some real bullshitting, yo. What the fuck happened between y'all down there? Tre probed in a frustrated tone.

He had been calling Vee and texting him. He had only gotten one reply: "Tell him yourself."

After that, nothing. Vee had returned no calls and no more texts.

"Nothing," Tito shrugged. "I kicked it with him on the way to the airport, not even a twenty-minute ride. I told him me and you was gonna stay outta they beef. Damn! I did tell him you brought me in on the company. He seemed vexed, but I ain't think it was that serious."

Tre shook his head.

"Evidently it was, yo."

"I mean, like, what the fuck? Especially after what you tellin' me now. Maybe it's for the best," Tito surmised.

"How you figure that?" Tre quizzed.

"The look that passed between the two old friends said it all. Tre sighed hard.

"Goddamn, Tito." It was all Tre could say because he saw Tito's point and hated the fact that he agreed.

"I'm sayin', fam, this the nigguh father we talkin' about. True indeed, he just found out, but you said yourself he was supposed to tell me. Why didn't he? Somethin' held him back from pourin' me a drink and that same something could make him feel a certain way after the nigguh done, see that? Now, where would that put us in the nigguh mind?" Tito reasoned, making his point clear.

"I'm just sayin', T, the nigguh a good nigguh. He young and hotheaded, but he solid," Tre replied, trying his best not to face the inevitable.

"From what I see, I agree. But he had to slump a few good nigguhs because the circumstances called for it," Tito reminded him. "It's the life we live."

"Used to live. At least for me, yo. At least until now," Tre answered.

"Maybe for me too soon enough. Wit' this deal on the table with Vanya, what we stand to make, we … well, I won't need this shit," Tito remarked.

"Speakin' of Vanya, what up with her and Vee? I musta missed a lot in Miami. Shortie keep blowin' me up tryin' to get at Vee. I keep tellin' her I'll let him know, but she persistent as fuck," Tre shook his head.

Tito was vexed. He hated for anything to get in the way of his plan for Vanya and the Charles family. What Tre said made killing Vee that much more necessary.

●●●●●●

"It's going down, but I didn't see our man," Hardy said into the Bluetooth of the burn-out.

"Then he only sent a team," Vee answered, driving along the highway on his way to Goldsboro.

"Fuck a team! I want him!" barked Hardy.

Vee told him exactly what to do, then hung up. The call confirmed it all for Vee. Ty had broken Karrin down. The phone call plus her guilt made her give in. Now that she knew Vee was Guy's son and that she had told him what he had done, it felt like the ground had opened up beneath her feet. And her safety net, Vee, turned out to be a spider's web, waiting for her to fall into it. From there, it was only a short step to letting Ty convince her to set Vee up. A few minutes after Hardy had told Vee a ten-man team had taken position in the parking lot and in Karrin's apartment, his phone rang again.

It was Karrin. He smiled and answered.

"What up? he asked, his demons straining to release.

"It's … it's the baby, Vee. I fell!" Karrin cried.

Vee shook his head at her treachery. It sounded real.

"Just be calm. I'ma call 9-1-1," he said.

"She quickly replied, "No! I-I-I don't want … Vee, you know why I'm here. I don't know if it's a warrant. Where are you?"

Damn she think quick, he thought.

"You want me to come?"

"I need you, Vee, the baby needs you."

"I'm closer than you think," he replied and hung up.

Karrin turned to one of the gunmen.

"I think he on his way."

"You think? Where he say he was at?"

"Close."

A few minutes later they learned how close. The eight dudes posted up outside had good position. Hardy and his five-man team just had better position. The AK-47s, SK-47s, 223s, and mini-14s erupted like the Middle

East came to Maryland. It took Ty's team totally by surprise. The bursting of one of the dude's heads let the remaining seven know shit was real.

"What the fuck?" one of the two gunmen inside exclaimed. The other looked out the window and saw the spark from the muzzles, the exploding glass of car windows, and the mad scramble of his team.

As soon as she heard the first gunshot, Karrin knew she had fucked up.

"I'm closer than you think."

She should've known Vee wouldn't have fallen so easily. She remembered what he said when he first took her *in*.

"If you ever cross me, I'll kill you and Ty!"

She knew he had come to make good on her half of the threat.

Meanwhile, Hardy was in a zone. Two of his people had been killed, but he was oblivious to it. He moved recklessly but effectively, hardly using cover, but picking off those who were. He opened fire on the large bay window of Karrin's apartment, sending gunmen and Karrin to the floor, bullets exploding overhead.

Dro and two more dudes kicked in the back door. The first one through caught a rack of hot ones from one of the gunmen, but by that time, Hardy had climbed the porch, which gave him a perfect shot into the living room. Hardy blew the back of the gunman's head all over Karrin. She threw up. Dro ran up and put his gun to the other gunman's head. He was the only one left alive from Ty's team.

"Don't kill me, man!"

One of Hardy's people opened up the front door. Hardy came in.

"Where's Ty?" he gritted.

"I-I-In Bmore man! He waitin' for us in Bmore!" the gunman told him.

"You wanna live?"

The gunman nodded vigorously.

"Then this is what you gonna do," Hardy replied and then proceeded to tell the gunman what Vee had told him.

Ty answered his burn-out on the first ring.

"It's done."

"You sure?" Ty asked intensely, feeling a murderous joy just thinking of Vee dead.

"Yeah, he was fuckin' the bitch when we got here," the gunman confirmed, following Hardy's script to the T.

Ty's blood pressure went through the roof.

"Bring that bitch to me," he seethed.

"We on our way."

The gunman hung up.

"Let's go," Hardy hissed, snatching Karrin to her feet.

Ty was pacing the floor without even knowing it. Tre looked up from the Madden football game he was playing against one the security guards.

"You a'ight lil' cuz?" Tre asked, glancing at Ty, then back at the screen.

"Yeah, yo, I'm Gucci," Ty replied. "I'ma step outside for a sec.

Tre nodded. Ty walked out of Tre's office.

"Yo, the nigguh say Ty at some porn studio in Bmore! We got that bitch-ass nigguh now!" Hardy exclaimed with a maniac's excitement. Vee's whole body tensed up. There was only one porn studio in Bmore Ty would have any reason to be at. The words of Vee's dream came back to him vividly.

"Always go with the odds," Tre said.

"Yo, Vee? You heard me?" Hardy called out.

"Yeah, yeah. Fo' sho'. Let me know when it's done. Anybody get in the way, don't play wit' 'em," Vee seethed, hoping Tre tried to bring in Brolic.

"I never do," Hardy laughed, then hung up.

⚫⚫⚫⚫⚫⚫

Ty was sick. Karrin was fucking Vee? He couldn't wait to get his hands on her. Not only had she run to his enemy, she tried to hide the fact that she'd been laying in the nigguh's arms?! Fucked this nigguh?! Sucked his …

"I'll kill her," he said.

Love or no love, she had crossed a line, and there was no coming back. Two sets of headlights made a right coming towards the warehouse. He knew it was them. Ty just didn't know which them it really was.

"Bitch, stay low 'cause I really don't give a fuck if you catch a stray one," Hardy warned her.

Karrin nodded vigorously. She was scared to death, but she was just as scared for Ty. He was a sitting duck.

As they turned the corner, she could see a lone figure standing in the parking lot of the warehouse. Her heart told her it was Ty. Her mind raced, and her survival tactics kicked in.

She was low behind the seat. Dro sat next to her, cocking his weapon and not paying any attention to her. She slid her hand in her pocket. She felt over the face of the phone with her thumb like the blind reading Brail. She found what she hoped was the send button. Desperately, she tried to remember the last person she called—Vee!

Who was before Vee?

Ty.

She clicked down one number and pressed send. They were nearing the parking lot. She hoped he would understand.

Ty glanced down at the ringing phone with a scowl. He looked at the screen.

Karrin?

He frowned. She was supposed to be in one of the cars turning into the parking lot. Why was she calling?

"Hello," he growled.

No response. Faint voices.

His street instincts screamed shit wasn't right.

The two cars turned in the parking lot.

"Kill the high beams," Hardy told the driver as he put his window down and laid the muzzle of the 223 on the doorsill.

The high beams glared in Ty's eyes a second before he reached for his gun on his waist. Everything in him screamed setup! The phone call, no response, the last-minute high beams. Ty was on point. Unfortunately it was too late.

"Remember me?" Hardy exclaimed, letting his automatic rip.

The moment Hardy pulled the trigger, it was the

climax of his life. Better than sex, more relief than the governor's last-minute call to stay the execution. It wasn't just revenge, it was pure retribution.

A line of bloody spurts cut across Ty's midsection. At the same time, Ty let off three struts, one sparking off the hood of the car. The second two hit the driver in his head and neck. He slumped forward and the car crashed into the building. Before it completely stopped, Hardy was out and firing.

"You fucked up, niggah! You shoulda killed me!" Hardy laughed.

They had caught Ty in the open. Ty fired back, but one of Hardy's boys let the AK-47 spit wildly. Three more shots hit Ty in his right side, spinning him around and dropping him. He used the last of his energy to roll behind a parked car.

Three security guards came busting through the door, pistols in hand. Hardy dropped the first with three to his chest, but the other two took cover and fired back. They were ex-marines and expert marksmen. One picked Dro off with a head shot halfway across the parking lot.

Hardy's 223 was empty. He crouched and sprinted for the cars. The remaining members of his team did the same. Hardy snatched open the back door of the second car and eyed Ty's gunman.

"How the fuck did he know?!" Hardy bassed, frustrated and confused as to how Ty got on point so quickly.

Even if he had an answer, Hardy didn't give him a chance to give it. He put the barrel of his .38 snub to his ear and let off three to the dome, then slung his lifeless body to the ground. Hardy got in and punched the back of the driver's seat.

"Go! Go! Go!!!"

Hardy and his team peeled out as more security guards and Tre came out, ready for war.

"Fuck!"

"Yo, Tre, over here! Call an ambulance. It's Tito's little cousin!" a security guard called out.

Tre ran over as he called and saw Ty. He looked bad. Blood everywhere. He was unresponsive. He looked dead. After he called 9-1-1, his mind settled on one name: Vee.

There was no doubt in his mind. He just didn't know what Ty had tried to do to Vee and that he had used the studio to orchestrate it. All Tre knew was Vee had brought it to him. It only confirmed what Tito said.

"Yeah, young nigguhs, you fuckin' with the pros now," Tre whispered menacingly.

⬤⬤⬤⬤⬤⬤

Ty was dead.

That was what Hardy had told Vee. He hadn't told him that Ty somehow peeped the setup. He didn't tell him about the blood bath. All he said was, "It's done, big homey. I'll hit you when I get back."

Vee entered the ranch to convey that message to the man he felt had to have allowed it, if not ordered it himself. In Vee's mind, Guy had to be involved. He thought Ty wouldn't move on him without Guy's approval, especially since Guy had all but said that.

After his maid opened the door and showed him to the kitchen, Vee thought of Ty. He wasn't glad or sad. He felt nothing. Ty had been one of his closest friends and one of his coldest enemies. Vee took no pride in being the winner of the beef, nor did he regret it. As he walked behind the maid, he quietly pulled his pistol, keeping it in the hand behind his back.

When he entered the kitchen, he found Guy and Shantelle. Something was burning. Vee could smell it and see the smoke wafting toward the ceiling. Shantelle was laughing so hard she had tears in her eyes. Guy looked up when Vee came in.

"Hello, Victor. I wasn't expectin' you tonight," Guy remarked, feeling a glimmer of hope that maybe Vee was coming around.

Shantelle wiped her eyes.

"I'm sorry, baby, but you do everything so well, it's good to see you look totally clueless!" she laughed again.

She came around the kitchen island and kissed Vee on the cheek. She automatically knew something was wrong.

"Victor? What's wrong?" she asked, her laughter gone.

Vee only nodded in Guy's direction.

"Ask him."

Now Guy sensed it too.

"What's going on?" Guy probed.

Vee looked at him dead in the eye and replied coldly, "I killed Ty."

Shantelle gasped and covered her mouth.

"Oh, my God, Victor. Why?"

"Because they tried to kill me."

Guy braced himself on the counter. His temperature was boiling "I tried, Shantelle. I tried to embrace thi—"

Vee cut him off with laughter.

"Embrace me?! You sit here laughin' in my mother's face while you send your sons to do your dirty work! Well, the joke's on you, nigguh! I won!"

Guy started to step around the island, but Vee put his arm at his side, revealing the gun.

"Victor, no!" Shantelle screamed, grabbing his free arm. "Please, baby!"

"So now you come to kill me?"

"That's up to you."

Guy shook his head. First Kev and now Ty. Guy tried to make sense of it.

"What do you mean he tried to kill you?"

"You already know."

"Tell me!" Guy barked so loudly it shook the patio glass behind him.

"He tried to set me up using Karrin," Vee replied and then the irony of the situation hit him. "Just like he did you."

Guy looked at him in total confusion, but a small part of his psyche knew exactly what Vee was talking about.

"Set who up?"

"You funny, huh? I guess Ty was both our enemies."

"What are you talking about, Victor?" Shantelle quizzed.

"All this time, thinkin' it had something to do with tryin' to kill you, thinkin' it was the Wolf Pack. The whole time it was your own seed. And the bitch that gave birth to him," Vee explained.

Guy leaned against one of the stools in front of the island. He didn't want to believe it, but that small part of him that listened to Vee's words was the small part that always knew. He had played the game too long not to recognize when a move was being made. He saw it in Debra. He sensed it in Ty after Debra's death. He just refused to accept it.

"You're lyin'," he whispered, defeated.

"For what? Why should I lie? I'm holdin' the gun," Vee reasoned with gangsta logic.

Seeing Guy sitting here, shoulders sagged, not denying Vee's words, Shantelle asked, "What ... bitch, Guy?"

Guy didn't respond. Instead, he looked at Vee.

"Karrin? How?"

Instead of answering, Vee pulled out his burnout and called Hardy.

"Yo."

"Put her on the phone."

"Vee, I love him. I'm sorry," Karrin said as soon as she got on the phone. It was like she was saying no matter what happened, she didn't flip on him, she just stayed loyal to Ty.

"Then ain't no hard feelings for either one of us. I got somebody here need to holla at you. Tell him everything, you understand?"

No response.

"Do you—"

"Is it Guy?"

This time Vee didn't answer. Karrin took a deep breath.

"Okay."

Vee extended the phone. Guy looked at it, then at Vee, then he took the phone. He never said a word the whole conversation. The whole time she told him, detail for detail, how Debra got Brah involved and how she got involved. How she wore contacts and changed up just enough to play the position Debra needed her to play. She told the story without emotion, without trying to blame Debra. The only time she pleaded was for Ty.

"I swear to you, Guy. He didn't know! He-he only found out when he found Debra with Brah and, you know, he was just covering for his mother and ... for me."

Guy had heard enough. He handed the phone back to Vee. He put it back in his pocket. Shantelle approached Guy.

"Say her name, Guy," Shantelle stated calmly, firmly, and coldly.

Guy looked up at her but couldn't hold her gaze.

"Say it, Guy. Say her name. Say the name that cost me twenty years of my life, two sons, and now the best thing that ever happened to you. Be man enough to say her goddamn name," Shantelle spat.

He looked at her with the firm strength of a dying man.

"Debra."

Shantelle wanted to slap the shit out of him, but the pain in his eyes touched her heart, so she did something much worse: she walked out. Guy couldn't blame her. He didn't attempt to stop her. He looked at Vee. "You came to shoot, so shoot."

He and Vee eyed each other across the island, and for only the third time in his life he felt remorse. Remorse for the fact that Vee didn't know who had taken more, him or Debra.

"I got what I came for," Vee replied. Then he walked out.

For the first time in a long time, Guy was alone, left only with what he cared about most: himself.

CHAPTER 47

When Tre told Tito what happened to Ty and who did it, Tito thought like Vee, only in reverse. If Vee hit Ty, Guy had to have allowed it, if not ordered it. If he could do that to his own son, and if he was willing to be a pawn for the Feds, what wouldn't he do?

Tito didn't hesitate to press the button, and the string he pulled was Gloria's.

"It's time," was all he said when he called.

She understood instantly.

"Tito, I don't think I can do it," she pleaded feebly.

"Then don't," he replied and hung up.

The ultimatum was clear. She knew it was time to go see Pam.

Gloria parked her Benz in the driveway behind the Lincoln MKZ with a small sign in the back window that said "God Loves." She looked at the house. It was in a quiet but comfortable neighborhood in Yonkers. The house was modest but well kept. It looked and felt like a home.

Pam's husband, James, answered the door. He didn't know Gloria, nor did she know him, but they knew of one another. The conversation was cordial. Then he led her through the house to the backyard. On her way, she saw pictures of a teenage boy who played high-school football and a grown daughter, a financial analyst for Goldman Sachs. They were Gloria's nephew and niece, whom she'd never met. It had been that long.

She stepped outside into the backyard to find Pam on her hands and knees, weeding her flower garden.

"Hello, Pam," Gloria greeted in an even tone.

Pam looked up. Gloria had called, so it wasn't a surprise, but the look in Pam's eyes showed she hadn't really expected Gloria to follow through. The last time she had seen Gloria was the family reunion in Aruba, where Gloria had all but wished death on her.

Pam stood up. She took off her gloves and smiled.

"How are you, Gloria? You're looking well," Pam commented.

Pam had gained some weight and her hair had grayed considerably, but looked happy, comfortable because she was loved. Gloria may've still been runway diva-ish, but she lacked and envied Pam's glow of love.

The moment was awkward, but Gloria hugged her anyway.

"Be careful," Pam giggled. "Don't wanna get you dirty."

Gloria shrugged and joked, "Helps the economy — keeps the cleaners in business."

They shared an awkward laugh, then sat on a sculptured stone bench in the middle of the garden.

"You have a beautiful garden," Gloria said.

"Thank you, but you should've saw it about four years ago. It looked like who dunnit and why!" Pam laughed.

They made small talk. Gloria felt Pam out and Pam wondered what Gloria was really there for. She knew her sister well, despite the more than twenty-year estrangement.

"Glory Bell," Pam smiled, using the nickname their grandmother used to call her, talk to me," she said, placing her hand on Gloria's. "I could always tell when something was bothering you."

Gloria dropped her head and fiddled with her fingers, then replied, "I messed up, big sis. I really messed up this time. Remember Mama used to say the hardheaded have to feel it to believe? Well, I believe it."

Pam took her hand.

"What is it? Money? A place to stay? We don't have much, but whatever I can do, Lord willin', it's done," Pam assured her, concern coloring her eyes.

It touched Gloria's heart that after all the years of absence because of hatred, Pam still responded without hesitation. It brought tears to her eyes.

"I'm so sorry, Pam," Gloria sniffled. "I'm sorry."

"For what?"

"For … Eddie," Gloria replied, wiping her eyes.

"Eddie?" Pam echoed. "What about …" she began to say, then her voice trailed off.

"It was Guy, Pam," Gloria admitted. "It was Guy, and I've known since Mama's funeral."

Pam dropped her head, shook it slowly, then looked back at Gloria.

"All this time, Gloria. All this time you knew? Why, Gloria?" Pam stressed.

"I loved him, Pam," she answered. "It hurt me to know, to carry that round, but, Pam, without Guy — I didn't want to live without him. I told Tito. He was beyond mad. If he would've killed me and Guy I, could not have blamed him, but what he wants me to do, I can't. I physically can't," Gloria emphasized, gripping her hand.

"What does he want you do?"

"Kill Guy. Or he'll kill me," Gloria told her.

Pam got up from the bench, shaking her head. "Lord have mercy. It never ends," Pam remarked painfully.

Gloria got up and approached her.

"I need you, Pam. Lord knows I do. I can't kill nobody, especially not Guy! I knew what he did was wrong, what I did was wrong, but this isn't the way to make it right! If-if you would talk to Theresa and just tell her, she'll listen to you, Pam," Gloria suggested.

Pam thought for a moment, then looked at Gloria and calmly replied, "No."

"No?"

"I won't get involved. Now, if it's money you need to … to get away or you need someplace to go, James' family in Chicago —"

Gloria's snicker cut her off.

"Money is the last thing I need. I got enough to go anywhere I want in the world and live like the best. But what's the point? I won't have my family, my friends, my life. I'll have nothing to make life worth living," Gloria explained passionately.

"Maybe that's the price you pay. When Kane killed Abel, he too was cast off. Maybe you need to be cleansed," Pam suggested solemnly.

"Cleansed? And purged too?" Gloria quipped bitterly. "Believe me, Pam, if I could talk to Theresa myself, I would. I know she'd put an end to this foolishness, but the way she looks up to me, the trust ..." Gloria shook her head. "I'd rather Tito do what he said he'd do to me, than see pain in that woman's eyes after all she's been through."

Pam took a deep breath and said with resolve, "My offer still stands, Gloria. I would give you my last dime, but I won't get involved with this devilment."

"So you'd rather see me become a killer or dead?" Gloria stressed.

You wished it on me. Now how does it feel, Pam thought. But she silently repented and said, "Only God can help you."

Gloria smiled and replied, "That's what I came here for. Good-bye, Pam."

As Gloria walked out of the backyard, Pam started to call her back and hold her because deep in her heart she knew she would never see Gloria again.

⬤⬤⬤⬤⬤⬤

Ty and Kev loved to go to New York for the summer. They had done it for as long as they could remember. After school let out Gloria packed them up and took them to Harlem.

As they got older, they would go on their own so they could hang with their cousin Tito. They idolized Tito. He had a swag that they both jacked, modified, and made their own.

Tito, in turn, loved his little cousins and took them everywhere, teaching them the is and outs of the game before they were old enough to play it.

"If I gave ya'll both a hundred dollars right now, what would you do with it?" Tito quizzed them.

"Jordans!" they both agreed.

"Then you'd be a customer, not a hustler. It's okay to have fly shit, but let the game pay for it. Now, say you take that hundred and buy mad candy and cookies, shit like that, and sold it all and made two hundred. Now you can have a hundred, but who paid for your Jordans?"

"The game," Kev answered.

"Customers," Ty replied.

"Exactly. That's how you have your cake and eat it too," Tito winked, dropping the first of many jewels on them.

The last summer they came to Harlem was when Kev was 17 and Ty had just turned 15. Tito had taken them school shopping on 125th, and they were balling out of control. They had the stacks Gloria gave them plus the clout of being with Tito. He was like a celebrity on 1-2-5, so when store owners saw his face, they rolled out the red carpet.

"I'm telling' you, Tito, man, Pops just don't understand," Ty griped. "We ready! The family need us, but he keep treatin' us like we lil' nigguhs."

"Ya'll is lil nigguhs," Tito joked, but neither cracked a smile. "On the real, I feel you. But Uncle Guy been around for a minute. If he say you ain't ready, then be easy."

"It ain't about that, yo. He just tryin' to protect us. In his eyes, we might never be ready, " Kev remarked.

Kev's words made Tito remember his mother's eyes when she told him to get out. He stopped walking and looked at both of them.

"Unk is just tryin' to keep ya'll from making a big

mistake. The game ain't for everybody. Now, I'm askin' both of ya'll to think about this. Don't just do it because I do it or Unk do it or because this shit look cool. Do it because you have to, because you want to see your own limits and enforce them and you ready and willing to accept the consequences."

It sounded like an oath to their young ears. The proper response seemed like "I do."

They both looked at each other, then back at Tito.

"Ain't shit to think about. I'd rather go to hell on my own than go to heaven followin' another nigguh, yo," Kev replied, using something Tito told them a long time ago.

Tito laughed."Okay, young gangsta, follow me," Tito told them, meaning every aspect of the phrase.

That summer was like Game 101. Tito showed them how to structure an organization, from the street soldiers to the lieutenants. He showed them how shifts should be organized, how money houses and stash houses should always be kept separately. He taught them hands-on things like how to cook coke, how to cut it, and how to tell how it's been cut.

"I know the Simmonses are known for dope, not coke, but my point is to know every aspect because a motherfucka that cut you back is just like an accountant cookin' the books. Either way you losin' money," Tito schooled them.

By the end of the summer, their eyes had been opened to a whole new world. The only world they would ever know.

"Now you know, but here is where you will show it," Tito had said, taking them to an arcade he had on the East Side. It was a hangout for teenagers called the Fun House. Ty and Ken would take the whole concept, including the name, back to N.C. and establish their first trap, but with one modification.

"Here I sell chips, candy, games. I keep it clean, and it gives me clout with the neighborhood. This is how you learn the ropes. Go home, open up a little spot like this. Keep it clean, build a network, know who's who, and then branch off into … other things," Tito explained.

"Why wait? A spot like this wouldn't jump in the borough unless nigguhs could cop that exotic and X pills out the back door," Kev surmised.

"Fo' sho'," Ty agreed, then turned to Tito. "So how 'bout it, cuz? What's the numbers on exotic and pills?"

Tito smiled.

"If I do this, Unk can never know."

"That goes without sayin'."

"Never."

"Never."

Guy would never know. Guy may've made Kev and Ty bosses, but it was Tito who first made them players.

A few moments later, one of Tito's workers ran up, out of breath.

"Yo! I'm glad I caught up with you!" he huffed. "Shit just popped off with your man at the Polo Grounds."

Tito frowned.

"My man who?"

"That nigguh Slice. Them Blood nigguhs just left him!"

"What the fuck happened?" Tito bassed, vexed that anybody would fuck with his paper.

The dude looked at Kev and Ty.

"These my people, yo. You can talk freely," Tito assured.

"I'm tellin' you, God, you ain't gonna like it."

"What I don't like is you beatin' around the bush."

"The twins … they did it."

"The twins who?!"

"Your twins, God, your sisters!"

Asia and Brooklyn were 16-year-old tomboys. They did everything rough. They went from fighting each other to fighting other kids, boys and girls. When they reached the age where weapons were used, they didn't hesitate to slash faces to make points.

Tito was at his wit's end.

"Like raisin' two goddamn boys!"

The twins were just coming into their beauty, but beauty was the last thing on their minds. They started hanging with a click of Blood chicks in Lincoln Projects. They weren't Blood yet, but they were close enough.

He worked for Tito's people. A lieutenant in the Polo Grounds. He went to Riker's Island and became Blood on the Island. He also told on some Bloods on the Island, so they called the streets and made him food, meaning he could be eaten.

The big homey gave them a mission.

"You do this and I'll bring you home," he offered, and the twins readily accepted.

Despite the fact that they were girls, and despite the fact that they were teens, they lacked remorse. Once they decided to do something, regardless of the outcome, they felt no regrets. Therefore, taking a life for the first time was no more a major decision than the first time they sliced a bitch's face open with a box cutter or the first time they burned ants.

That day Slice was the ant they burned.

Coming out of the corner store near the Polo Grounds, he was on point, but he was distracted by the pretty smile of the gorgeously radiant female on his left. Because of her, he didn't see the equally gorgeous female approach on his right. When he did, he had to do a double take.

Same face, same beauty, but only one bore a smile. The other bore arms. Then heaven and hell united to end his existence. Twin Desert Eagles to match the twin assassins.

Close range. Two emptied clips. Slice was so dead he didn't even twitch. Closed casket. End of story.

Tito arrived on the Polo Grounds.

The big homey had just found out Slice was a part of Tito's larger circle. He already knew the twins were his sisters. He thought that fact could save him, but the look in Tito's eyes made him seriously doubt it.

"Where they at?" Tito growled, then approached the big homey with Kev and Ty.

"Yo, T, my word, I ain't know that you fucked with that nigguh," the big homey replied, trying to mitigate the damage.

Tito stepped up closer.

"But you knew they were my sisters!"

The big homey didn't like being raised on in his hood in front of his people, but now was not the time to stress etiquette.

"They came to us, yo."

"Then you shoulda come to me," Tito retorted.

Asia and Brooklyn came out of the building wearing red bandanas around their necks. Tito approached them. Even though both were scared of their brother, they were too stubborn to run.

"We-we don't know — " Brooklyn began.

Tito responded by snatching the bandanas from their necks so forcefully it gave Asia burn marks and made Brooklyn stumble to the ground.

"Get up," he hissed. And when she did, he added, "If this is what you wanna do, if this is what you wanna be, then the only goddamn flag you rep is our last name! That's your bloodline! Are you clear?"

"No doubt."

"No question."

"Now go get in the car," he ordered, then went back over to the big homey.

Tito extended the flags to him in an iron grip. The big homey knew if he didn't take them back, it would be war. Besides the fact that Tito controlled states from Ohio to Boston to Maryland, Tito was also feeding several other Blood sets in New York. Lack of unity could easily make big the homey food too. Therefore, he fell back and took the flags. Tito's eyes stayed still as he walked away with his family.

Vanya walked into Tre's office. Her appearance had been unexpected but not a surprise after the shootout. Tre tightened security at the studio, thinking Vee was behind it and didn't know what he would do next. Therefore, all visitors were first cleared by security. So when he got a call on the walkie-talkie saying Vanya Charles was there, he smiled at Tito, who also heard the transmission.

"Okay. Send her in."

When she entered, her eyes fell on Tito.

"I should've known you'd be here," she smirked knowingly.

"Meaning?" Tito replied, returning her smirk.

Vanya turned to Tre. "Since I can't seem to get anything out of you over the phone, I thought I'd come and ask you in person. Where is Victor?" she asked.

Vanya Charles was a woman used to getting what she wanted. She wasn't spoiled. She was just supremely confident that whatever she wanted, she deserved. She didn't necessarily want Vee, but the thrill of the pursuit made her want him to know she could have him if she wanted. At least that's what she told herself.

"Eh, me and Vee had a little difference of opinion, and he decided to … step back for a while, you know? Reassess our relationship," Tre said diplomatically.

Vanya understood. She was well versed in the ability to read between the lines.

"This reassessment wouldn't have anything to do with the tighter security, the bullet holes in the door or the … incident the other night, would it?" Vanya asked.

"Totally unrelated," Tito answered, rising from the couch and coming over to her. "But it's good to know nothin' gets by you," he added sarcastically.

"You of all people should know me, Tito, so you know I must know who I do business with," she replied, trying to provoke him.

"All of them?" he retorted, letting her know he spoke innuendo too.

Vanya laughed because she like sharp people.

"Only the interesting ones," she answered. Then she said to Tre, "So … is Vee a part of Red Light Films or what?"

Tre hesitated.

"That's hard to say, but Red Light as a company is committed to doing business with Charles Communications."

"Business? Do you believe in trust, Tre? I mean, in a business sense," she added.

"True indeed."

"So any … internal differences in upper management are a serious matter? I mean, difference of opinion is good for gambling but not necessarily good business, wouldn't you agree?"

Tre subtly glanced at Tito. Tito subtly nodded.

Vanya subtly ignored the subtlety.

"I guess it wouldn't be a problem if I gave you Vee's number so you can see things for yourself," Tre conceded.

"Would you?" Vanya replied with sweet sarcasm. "That would be great."

Tre slid her Vee's number. She started for the door.

"Vanya," Tito said.

She looked back over her shoulder.

"That 'soon' is gettin' to be like tomorrow, huh?" Tito quipped.

She smiled with the sensuality of a cat and replied, "At least tomorrow gives us something to look forward to."

●●●●●●

Vee was back in Miss Sadie's house. It was raining outside. Hard. He stepped in front of the full-length mirror and looked at his reflection. He saw Kev. It was his clothes, his movements, his facial expressions, but he saw Kev's face, Kev's body.

"What the fuck?!" Vee exclaimed and watched Kev's lips move in sync.

"What do you want?"

"You ain't me!'

"I ain't you!"

"Yo!"

Each statement he spoke bounced uselessly off the mirror. Kev was only a reflection, except for his eyes. So Vee stopped talking. He stopped moving and resisting and looked into the eyes in the mirror.

The seed. The seed is your last chance. Your last chance. The only way back.

"Suppose I don't want to come back?"

You will.

And then he woke up.

Vee thought about the dream as he and Hardy rode to take Karrin to Guy. He had called Guy and said, "She's pregnant with Kev's baby. You want her, yes or no?"

There was hesitation.

"Yeah," Guy replied, "bring her to me."

They agreed to meet on a quiet back road leading out of Mount Olive. Hardy drove while Vee rode in the back with Karrin.

"The baby is the only reason I'm alive, isn't it?" Karrin probed.

"Yeah," Vee answered without looking at her.

"Because of you or Guy?"

He didn't respond, but he thought of the dream.

"Is it true that he's ..." she began to ask, but the look in Vee's eyes deaded the rest of the sentence in her throat.

"Shut the fuck up," he hissed.

"Yeah, bitch, just be patient, you'll be dead soon," Hardy cackled.

"I just hope I get to beat that pussy one time before I kill you and that bastard in your goddamn belly!"

Hardy didn't see the look Vee shot him, but Karrin did and it told her all she needed to know.

The seed ...

As they neared Mount Olive, Hardy looked in the

rearview and asked, "Yo, Vee, after this, where we go from here?"

"I don't know."

"I'm sayin', dawg, no homo, but I fucks wit' you. You a real nigguh, and I know I'm a real nigguh, so real talk, who the fuck could stop us?! We could do big things if we wanted to," Hardy proposed.

"We'll talk about it after this. Make a right," Vee answered.

They turned the corner on the dark country road to an even darker stretch of nothing. The only light was the set of fog lights on the opposite side of the road. As they approached, Hardy tensed with anticipation.

"Yeah, Uncle Brah, this one for you," Hardy said, almost in a prayer-like tone.

The seed …

"Stop right here," Vee instructed him.

They stopped about 20 feet from the other car.

"Dead the lights."

"Wait here wit' the bitch. I'ma make sure the nigguhs ain't got us walking into a trap. When I signal, bring her," Vee explained.

"Come out blazin'?" Hardy asked, anxious to set it off.

"As soon as I step aside."

"Fo' sho'."

Vee got out. He could see Guy's silhouette leaning against the grill of the Benz. Vee approached, gun in hand.

"Where is she?" Guy asked.

"In the car with my man."

"What are we waitin' for? Some kind of guarantee? You think I'd set you up like you did Kev? Like you did Ty?" Guy questioned him with a solemn weight in his tone.

Right then Vee knew Guy wasn't alone. He could feel it. He knew he was probably in the scope as they spoke, but death was the furthest thing from his mind.

"Naw, naw, I don't want a guarantee, and I don't think you'd set me up," Vee responded.

"Then the next move is on you," Guy responded.

Vee studied Guy for a moment, then turned and signaled Hardy. The only thought in his mind was: Guy or Hardy.

If Hardy killed Guy, who would protect the seed in Karrin's belly? He knew his dream meant he had to make a choice, and he had to make it now.

As Hardy walked up, he knew there was no turning back. Hardy wouldn't leave without Guy's blood on his hands. No matter the outcome, Hardy was committed, so sparing Guy meant killing Hardy.

"Hello, Karrin," Guy greeted, letting her know her life was now firmly between his thumb and forefinger.

"I-I'm sorry, Guy," she sobbed.

He didn't even respond to Karrin's crocodile tears. Instead, he looked at Hardy.

"Vee, who is this?"

In that moment, action and reaction blurred into destiny. Vee stepped back, the signal Hardy was waiting for, but it didn't mean what he thought it meant.

"Young Bruh Hardy, nigguhs!" Hardy hissed and began to pull the gun from his back.

The words reached Guy's ears, but before anyone reached, Vee had his gun to the back of Hardy's head and his hand on Hardy's gun, disarming him.

"Don't move, nigguh," Vee told him calmly but firmly.

"Goddamn, dawg, not you too!" Hardy replied. The pain in his voice was deeper than betrayal; it was total defeat.

Hardy moved on two extremes: loyalty and revenge. He was like a pit bull. He was vicious, but once he attached, he didn't let go in love or war. He had attached to Vee just as he had attached to Kev. Both had betrayed him. Kev had cost him his family. Vee would cost him his life.

Guy's six-man team, including Hawk Bill, emerged from both sides of the road. Two Broncos high-beamed them. All guns were aimed at Hardy and Vee' except Hawk Bill's.

"Victor, what the hell is going on?!" Guy demanded to know.

"This is the nigguh that killed your wife, Ty's mother, and the nigguh I used to kill Ty. If you want him, he yours," Vee explained.

Guy looked from Vee to Hardy. Vee and Hawk Bill looked at each other. Hawk knew why Vee wanted to connect with Hardy. He hated that he had used him to kill Ty, but deep down, Hawk Bill couldn't blame him. But seeing Vee now told Hawk Bill his nephew understood gangsta justice well.

Hardy knew he was about to die, but he wasn't about to go out like a sucker.

"Fuck it. It is what it is. Whateva they paid you, dawg, I hope some bitch-ass nigguh get a lucky shot or forty to life in a box," Hardy said. "I ain't even mad at you," he said to Guy. "I murdered your bitch-ass son and his whore-ass mama squealed like a pig when I stuck the barrel in her pussy!" Hardy laughed.

Guy snatched Hardy's gun out of Vee's hand and stuck it in Hardy's mouth. Guy looked him in the eyes and blew his head off. Hardy slumped to the ground, and Guy hit him twice more in the face.

"Get this piece of shit outta here. And, Hawk, take this trflin' bitch back to the house," Guy ordered.

Hawk Bill looked at him and Vee.

"What about ya'll?"

"We're good," Guy assured him.

Guy and Vee, both with guns in hand, eyed one another evenly, but without malice, trying to make sense of everything.

The team packed up in both Broncos and pulled off, leaving Guy and Vee in the darkness, shadowed only by the Benz's fog lights.

"Hardy thought he was coming to kill me, didn't he?"

"Yeah."

Silence.

"So why did you change your mind?"

"I didn't."

Guy nodded. He knew Vee meant that killing Hardy had been his plan the whole time. Ever since Miami Vee knew that would be the outcome. The dream had only confirmed what was in his heart.

"Why?" Guy wanted to know.

Vee could've said because of Shantelle or because of the baby. Instead, he said the reason he had been struggling with and was just able to admit.

"'Cause you my father."

Guy couldn't find the words to respond, and Vee felt no need to say more. The only thing left for Vee to do was walk away, and the only thing for Guy to do was stop him.

"Vee."

He turned around.

"Follow me to the house."

Hawk Bill closed the door of the guest room and locked it, leaving Karrin alone in the world. Her first impulse was to laugh. There was no need to lock her in the room. If anything, they should lock her out. It was like locking the gates of heaven. For what? She remembered Guy's words on the way to Kev's funeral: "Karrin, you will always be part of this family. Never forget you're a Simmons."

She intended to fully cash in on that promise. Not only was the life inside of her the reason she was live, it was the reason she would also be taken care of. Karrin mourned Ty's death. A part of her died as well, but not the part that made her a survivor. Only the part that loved.

"The maid will show you to one of the guest rooms. We'll talk in the mornin'," Guy told him as he headed out of the living room. Vee glanced around the room. He didn't know what it was Guy wanted to talk about in the morning. For Vee, there was nothing to talk about. He didn't even know why he had even come back with Guy. There was no way they could get past the past. Vee had killed both his brothers, Guy's sons, and Guy was a rat in Vee's eyes. Neither would be able to see beyond that.

Vee decided to just leave. Walk away. Let Tito or Tre or whoever do what Guy's hand called for. Father or no father, Vee couldn't condone snitchin' and that's what he felt like he'd be doing if he didn't leave or didn't kill Guy himself. The latter was out. Vee had done a 180. He could no longer stomach killing his own father, but neither could he stomach what his father was.

Vee started for the door, but a glistening in the corner of his eye caught his attention. It had come as he walked by the drawn curtains. He backed up a step to the space between the two curtains and saw the glisten again.

Vee stepped to the window and held the curtain back with his hand. The lights inside the pool shimmered to the surface and a gentle breeze caused the soft ripples to retract light. He forgot everything and thought of Taheem.

Guy stood in his bedroom, looking at a picture of Ty and Kev when they were both toddlers. The memory made him smile, but reality made his heart ache.

He wasn't upset with Ty. Caught between the man who raised him and the woman that bore him, he made the natural choice. He didn't blame Debra. She had crossed a man to be with him, then used that same man to cross him. She may not have been slicker than Guy, but she was more committed to being slick, and in the game of life, the race doesn't always go to the swift — it goes to the steady. Debra hadn't changed, he had.

He blamed himself, and for the first time, he regretted the direction he had taken his life. Regretted that he hadn't been strong enough to be his own man, gone to college, and become an "uppity nigguh." The thought made him chuckle. Dr. Guy Simmons, Professor Guy Simmons, Ph.D. Any Guy Simmons besides the Guy Simmons he had become as a result of his father's frown.

But he didn't blame Willie either. Guy had lost everything, but it was his own fault. He watched Vee come out onto the balcony and sit down by the pool. By the law of the jungle, Vee had proven to be the fittest.

He was flesh of his flesh and blood of his blood, but he was also the destroyer of Guy's dynasty.

Guy turned around to his dresser and picked up the cordless and dialed a number.

"Daddy, we need to talk," Guy said pinching the bridge of his nose.

Vee stared at the water, thinking of Taheem. It was like he could see his little man tottering toward him as the water was calling him, embracing him, sucking him under, taking him away forever. The thought triggered one of Cat, past and present, then he thought of the Wolf Pack, Mike G, Rome, Banks, Rico, Pappy, even Ty. But where would he go? What would he do?

He no longer trusted Tre, so Red Light Films was no longer an option. His choices seemed limited and the thought drained him. He sat for what seemed like minutes, but was really hours. He was so alone he didn't hear Guy come up behind him.

"You hungry?" Guy asked.

Vee glanced halfway over his shoulder.

"Naw, I'm good."

"You always get up this early?"

"I never went to sleep."

"Me neither," Guy replied. "Take a ride with me."

Vee looked at him.

"Where?"

"I got somebody I want you to meet."

Vee looked at his watch.

"It's 5 o'clock in the mornin'."

Guy laughed.

"Yeah, I said the same thing."

Vee stood up.

"Check it out, yo, I think I should tell you—"

Guy held up his hand.

"Later. Whatever it is, it can wait, okay? Just give me today. One day. That's all I ask. Then you can tell me. Deal?" Guy asked, and then, for the first time, extended his hand.

Vee looked at it, then at Guy, then shook his father's hand.

As the sun rose, Guy and Vee traveled to a small out-of-the-way airport in Pikesville, where Guy kept his private G-4 stashed away.

Vee had never been on a private plane, so he couldn't help but be impressed by the luxury.

"This yours?" Vee questioned.

"The company's."

"What company?"

"I don't know, one of 'em," Guy replied.

They flew to Atlanta, refueled, then went to New Orleans. There was a stretch Mercedes limo waiting near the runway. As Guy and Vee neared the limo, the door opened. Guy ushered a reluctant Vee in, then got in behind him.

An elderly Chinese woman and a young Chinese

dude sat inside. Guy shook the dude's hand, then kissed the woman on the cheek.

"Mrs. Li Wu, I would like you to meet Victor, my son," Guy said.

Vee shook Wu's hand. He spoke to Mrs. Li in Chinese. Mrs. Li smiled and responded in French. She held her hand out limply. Vee took it. Her hand felt small and fragile in his.

"Mrs. Li says it is nice to meet you," Wu translated.

"Likewise," Vee nodded.

Wu turned to Guy.

"And what is the nature of this meeting you called for, Guy?" Wu inquired, getting down to business.

Guy helped himself to the wet bar.

"The future," Guy replied, pouring himself two fingers of Cognac.

"I see. Then I take it Victor is to be a part of it," Wu surmised.

Guy nodded and sipped. Wu spoke Chinese. Mrs. Li spoke French. Wu spoke again, then turned to Guy.

"Mrs. Li says this is very sudden. You are not ill, are you?"

"Well, as the old folks back home say, I'm sick and tired of being sick and tired," Guy chuckled. "I'm at a point in my life where I felt I had to prepare for the inevitable. Only legacies live forever."

"I understand," Wu acknowledged.

Besides, this isn't immediate. My son and I," Guy began and looked at Vee, "have a lot to discuss, but my course of action is final. Only the details must be worked out."

Wu translated, and Mrs. Li replied, looking at Vee.

"Mrs. Li says that power is inheritable, but wisdom not necessarily so. Your father has—how do you say—big shoes to fill. Can you fill them?" Wu probed.

Vee looked at Guy. This was totally unexpected. The whole scene felt surreal to Vee. It was clear what Guy was doing. Mrs. Li was his connect. The only thing he had inherited when Po' Charlie died. These were truly the keys to the kingdom Guy was offering Vee when he hadn't even expected to be let in the gate.

"I wear my own shoes," Vee replied without bravado, just matter factly. Guy chuckled. Wu smirked and translated. Mrs. Li looked at Vee and laughed softly.

"Oui," she said.

"Mrs. Li says the normal protocol for such matters must be adhered to, but that she will not object when the time comes," Wu informed them.

"Thank you for your time," Guy said, shaking Wu's hand and kissing Mrs. Li's. He opened the door and Vee got out. The limo pulled off.

Guy turned to Vee. "Look, I know you didn't expect this. I wrestled with it all night, but I know it's the right thing to do, even if it is sudden," Guy explained.

Vee had one question: "Why?"

Guy shrugged. "Because you're my son. You're all I got and by any standard you deserve it. How we got here is irrelevant, Victor. The point is we here now. We can't turn back. And no, this ain't about tryin' to make amends or some kind of compensation. Like I said, you mine and you deserve it, so it's yours if you want it."

It was a once-in-a-lifetime chance. This was not only a connect, it was the source that would make Vee the connect. It was a chance to stack millions and all he had to say was yes.

"No," Vee replied, looking Guy in the eyes.

"No??" Guy repeated, angry and hurt at the same time.

I can't take it wit' strings attached," Vee added.

"What the hell are you talkin' about?! Do you know who the fuck that was?!" Guy barked.

"The Feds?" Vee quipped.

"The who?!" Guys asked, confused.

"I know you an informant, Guy. I know you work for the Feds," Vee stated evenly.

Guy eyed him for a moment, then broke out laughing.

"An informant? Is that what you think?"

Guy laughed even harder. Vee was waiting for him to try and deny it.

"Me? Work for the Feds? Nigguh, the goddamn Feds work for me!" Guy boasted with bark.

Vee shook his head in disgust. "Ain't no different. A snitch is a snitch."

Guy shot him a look.

"Guy Simmons has never been a snitch, a rat, or a goddamn informant, ya hear? And I won't say it again."

Vee didn't back down.

"But you just said they were working for you! Fuck that supposed to mean?!"

"It means I'm so high up the food chain, it'll give most nigguhs nosebleeds! Make 'em dizzy form the goddamn heights!" Guy based, heated.

He looked around the airstrip even though no one was close to them. He checked his anger and lowered his tone. "The shit I get don't get smuggled in or snuck in. It flies in courtesy of the United States government on this level. It ain't about laws, it's about politics," Guy schooled him.

"So why your name come up as an informant?" Vee wanted to know.

"It'll come up the same way with the ATF, the DEA, and the Coast Guard. You know why? It means hands off. Everybody thinks I'm workin' for everybody else, and no one makes a move. Then when I got somebody I want moved, I want leaned on, or pushed back, they handle it for me," Guy answered.

Vee was back to disgust.

"And that ain't snitchin'? Get the fuck outta here," Vee spat dismissively. Guy took a deep breath and shook his head, thinking Vee had a lot to learn.

"Snitchin' is when you give someone up to save yourself. That I would never do. Look, you don't get to this level without playin' the game, and if this level ain't your goal, what you playin' for? Pablo Escobar, the Cartels all of 'em used the government. The government never uses us. That's the difference!"

Vee understood his point. He just couldn't agree.

Guy continued. "Besides, it works both ways. I can stop investigations just as fast as I can start one. Like the one in Durham."

Vee shot him a look.

"Yeah, I know about that. One word from me, and I can get it finished," Guy offered.

There was no way he would tell Vee had been the one that got it started in the Wolf Pack's direction.

"Fuck no," Vee replied.

"Victor, it's first degree mu —"

Vee cut him off.

"Guy, my word, stay the fuck outta my affairs! What you do is what you do, but that ain't me," Vee warned him.

Guy relented.

"Okay, Victor. If that's what you want."

Vee didn't respond. He brushed past Guy and headed for the plane. Resigned, Guy took a deep breath and followed him.

The flight back was long. Neither man spoke, both standing behind a wall of pride. It was nighttime when they got back. As Guy drove, sensing this was his last chance to reach Vee, he finally broke the silence.

"Look, Victor, I can understand how you feel about the politics of the game. Sort of like in Greek mythology, how the gods play by different rules. What I did today wasn't meant to change hands. I'm a young man, so I got a lotta years left," Guy chuckled, then glanced over at Vee. "I'd just rest a whole lot easier knowing my … my … our bloodline lived on."

Vee didn't say anything, but Guy could tell he was listening. He continued.

"At least let's get to know one another on a smaller scale. I know our connect is gone. With me, you don't have to worry about that. And if, God forbid, shit should get hot for you, I give you my word as a man and as your father that I won't do anything to stop it. You'll be free to do football numbers," Guy quipped sarcastically.

Vee looked at him.

"I'll think about it," Vee replied, though his tone said he wasn't interested. They pulled up at the ranch.

Guy noticed Hawk Bill's car was gone. He had told him to take Karrin to another location until she had the baby because Guy feared he might strangle the bitch. But he noticed another rental car parked behind Vee's rental. He wasn't worried because nobody could get this close without passing security, but it made him curious.

"Guess I got visitors," he remarked as he and Vee went inside.

The first thing he saw when he came in was the maid. She looked worried. She was wringing her hands nervously.

"I-I-I'm sorry, Mr. Simmons, but it's Mrs. Simmons. I told her you weren't here, but she said she'd wait and … and I could tell she had been drinking and … well, you know how Mrs. Simmons is," she explained nervously.

Guy chuckled.

"It's okay, Charlotte. Mrs. Simmons is always welcome here."

He figured Gloria was ready to come home. But then he thought about the fact that Vee was there. Out of respect for Gloria, he felt that they shouldn't meet like this. He turned to explain to Vee, but before he could, Gloria came out of his study. Her steps were subtly shaking the effects of the alcohol in her system. She wrapped her arms around Guy.

"Surprise, baby. Happy to see me?" she purred, kissing him, then sucking his bottom lip.

Guy shied away from kiss.

"Where you been, Glo, a liquor house? It ain't like you to be drunk," Guy remarked suspiciously.

"I ain't drrrunkk," she giggled, "I'm feelin' good. Come on upstairs and let me show you how good."

Gloria took Guy's hand and turned for the stairs. Her plan was to pamper him. Love him. Show him it was her he needed and vice versa, all in an attempt to convince him to take her and run. Run from the consequences and the mistakes of the past to an unknown future together. Her whole unconscious plea was, Give me a reason not to do it.

Instead, she saw Vee. She hadn't noticed him before. She just thought he was one of Guy's lackeys, but as she turned for the stairs, a flash of recognition made her pause and look again. She mistook the recognition for the memory it triggered and her attitude flipped from caressing to crimson.

"Who are you?" she exclaimed, her anger instantly boiling away her high.

Vee looked at Guy, allowing him to handle the situation.

"Glo, come on. Let's go upstairs. This is pointless," Guy responded, trying to smooth things over.

He took her hand, but she snatched away and slightly stumbled.

"Nigguh, you ain't man enough to tell me the truth? How 'bout you? You a goddamn man or you gonna lie too?! Who are you?!"

"I'm Vee," Vee answered calmly and fully realizing who Gloria was.

Gloria looked at Guy with pure hatred and disgust.

"And I came to give you a chance," she said, shaking her head. "Nigguh, you ain't shit. Ain't never been shit. And would've never been shit if it wasn't for my goddamn brother! Yeah, Vee, you just like yo' daddy. He killed his own brother too, brother-in-law," Gloria spat.

Guy had both fists balled, but he felt he owed Gloria at least a chance to vent. She was face to face with her son's killer, but even venting had its limits.

"Gloria, I know it's painful seeing Vee like this, but I'm warnin' — "

"Or what, Guy? Huh?" she laughed like she was finally free. "What else can you do to me?! Every time I think this too shall pass, you find another way to step all over me!"

"You're drunk!"

"Not anymore, baby," she shook her head. "I was drunk, blind, and crazy for 28 years, 7 months, and 16 goddamn days, but I ain't no more."

"Okay, Gloria, you had your say," Guy replied, attempting to grab her arm, but she moved away and pulled a .38 revolver our of her pocket.

"And I ain't finished!" she hissed, watching Vee and Guy. "Now, both of you, I'm scared and I'm mad, so do not fuckin' play wit' me! Put your guns on the floor now!"

Vee looked at Guy like, Is she serious? Guy was totally shocked. Gloria had never been this volatile, but he believed in his ability to handle the situation. He subtly nodded. He and Vee put their guns on the floor.

"Gloria, listen to me. You're dru — " he began to say, then thought better of it. "You're not thinkin' straight. I ... " Guy's voice trailed off as the realization hit him.

What was she doing with a gun in the first place.

Her smile read the confusion in his eyes.

"So now you know what I meant when I said give you another chance," Gloria clarified. "I came here for you, and I got something better."

She aimed the gun at Vee.

"You killed my son, you file son of a bitch, and now it's your turn," she hissed.

"Do what you do," Vee replied, challenging her to make good on the threat.

"Did Tito put you up to this too, Gloria? Like our little conversation about Ty?" Guy accused.

"Shut up!' Gloria spewed.

"Gloria, don't do this!" Guy boomed, trying to assume an authority he no longer had.

"I'm not, she smiled. "You are, Guy."

She was giving Guy the same ultimatum Tito had given her.

"Guy, I love you. You know that. Despite all you've ever done. But you're going to make this right. This one thing, Guy, that's all I ask," Gloria offered.

Here tone was firm, but underneath, she was begging. It was the same thing she had been asking for, only now it was at gunpoint.

"Glo," Guy began heavily, "I told you before that was what I won't do. Aiming a gun at me won't change it."

Guy stepped in front of Vee.

"Guy, you ain't gotta do that. She won't—" Vee began, but his words were cut short by gunshots.

The impulse that made her pull the trigger three times was the rage she felt seeing Guy step in front of Vee. In her delusional mind, that one act seemed to say she didn't matter, Kev didn't matter, their whole life didn't matter. She squeezed the trigger at a reality she couldn't accept, a reality represented by Guy's flesh. Two hit his stomach and one hit his heart, stopping it instantly and ending his life before his large frame slumped to the floor between Gloria and Vee.

"Pop!" Vee exclaimed without knowing he said it. The familiar twitch told the killer in Vee that Guy was gone.

"Don't move, motherfucka. You'll be with him soon enough," Gloria gritted.

"One of us will," he retorted angrily.

"This is for Kev, you piece of shit!" Gloria spat and raised the gun for a head shot. But when she looked back at Vee's face, it wasn't Vee she saw, it was Kev.

Her knees almost gave out. Her mind connected with why her earlier recognition had triggered the memory of Kev. Looking into Vee's eyes for the first time, she saw the same kind of eyes, the same facial structure, the same lips.

"No," softly escaped from her lips and her heart swelled. Her arm holding the gun began to tremble. Slowly but surely, Gloria's mind unclouded and the reality she had refused to accept hit her dead in the face.

"What have I done?" she whispered.

The energy drained from her body and she fell to her knees, her spirit being consumed by a grief she would never return from.

"Oh, my God, Guy! What have I done?! No, God, no! What have I done?!" she exclaimed, taking Guy's head in her lap.

Vee bent down and picked up the pistol. The cocking of the hammer made Gloria look up. Vee aimed the gun at her face.

"Do it! Do it! Finish the job! You see what you made me do?! You! It's your fault! You've destroyed this family!" Gloria sobbed, then added in a desperate mumble, "Please just finish the job."

Vee knew she was right. His mere presence had caused bloodshed. He could feel the demon laughing, "Just you and me, nigguh, just you and me!"

The price was getting harder to pay. He looked up and saw the maid watching, tears lining her cheeks and her hand over her mouth. Vee lowered the gun and turned away.

"Finish the job!" Gloria screamed, but Vee shut the door in her face, leaving her to shoulder the guilt alone.

Her world would never be the same. Everything she had was gone. Her family shunned her, Kev was dead, and now Guy was too. She was no longer a mother, a wife, a sister, an aunt. She was nobody in her grieving mind.

In that moment of her deepest despair, the only light in the enveloping darkness of her soul was the gleam of the gun under Guy's thigh.

She grabbed it like a drowning person would grab a rope.

As Vee got into the car, he heard the sound he had been expecting since he walked out. The sound of a single gunshot, followed by the piercing scream of the maid.

Gloria had finished the job herself.

CHAPTER 48

Cat entered the psychiatric ward ofJohns Hopkins Hospital. After searching endlessly, she had finally found Angelo. She needed him like she needed the heroin her body craved. He was her emotional stability. Without him she had been adrift, doing things for the drug she thought no human should be asked to do. And she didn't have Angelo to come back to afterwards. Cat didn't mind being used as long as she was loved.

She waited twenty minutes before a nurse finally escorted her to Angelo's room. Her heart was aflutter with anticipation.

"When can I take him home?" she asked the nurse as they walked.

"Mr. Thomas has suffered an extremely traumatic experience. You'll have to talk to the doctor."

Cat was prepared for anything besides what she found. When they opened the door, Angelo was lying on the bed in a fetal position. His back was to the door. He was rocking back and forth, and Cat could hear his muffled mumbles.

"He's been totally uncommunicative. He talks ... gibberish. Medically, there isn't an explanation as to why. The doctors are baffled," the nurse admitted.

She stood back while Cat approached the bed.

"Baby ... baby, it's me. It's Kitty," Cat said softly, using the name Angelo had given her.

She placed her hand softly on his shoulder.

"Everything's gonna be okay, daddy. Kitty's here and I ain't goin' nowhere," she vowed sincerely.

Angelo stopped rocking. His body tensed. He looked over his shoulder, wide-eyed. He let out an animalistic moan, hopped off the bed, and cowered in the corner, speaking in cursed tongues.

Cat was shocked. She didn't know what had happened.

"Daddy, it's me," she said with concern as she rounded the bed to approach him.

If Angelo could've gone through the wall, he would've. He banged and clawed the wall, babbling loudly, speaking clearly in his own mind but unaware of the incoherent babble coming out of his mouth.

"I'm afraid you're going to have to leave, Miss Richards," the nurse insisted, calling for assistance.

"But what's wrong?"

"No, Miss Richards!"

The nurse ran to Angelo, and he clung to her like a baby to a mother, eyes full of hateful terror as he looked at Cat.

One word came to mind: Vee.

Filled with scorn, she turned on her heels and walked out of the room, right into the arms of two white men.

"Excuse me," she huffed, trying to go around them.

One blocked her path.

"Kianna Richards?"

"Who?" she played dumb and again attempted to pass. Frustrated, she spat, "Get the hell outta my way!"

One of the men flashed a badge.

"Ms. Richards, Baltimore City police. We need to ask you a few questions."

Cat wondered how they knew who she was. Her mind was too frazzled to remember giving it at the front desk. The hospital was under instruction to inform the police immediately if Angelo received a visitor. That's why they had her wait twenty minutes—so they could monitor the visit and intercept the visitor. The Angelo crime had been too bizarre. The police showed special interest because they were scared a serial killer was starting up. Cat was the first break in the case and an even bigger break in another case.

"Am I under arrest?"

"Person of interest. Please come with us."

At the police station, they were cordial, and Cat was more than cooperative.

"Do you know of any enemies Mr. Thomas may —"

"Vee."

"My baby fa- … ex-baby father."

"Ex?"

No response.

"What's his real name?"

"Victor Murphy from Durham, N.C."

They ran his name. They ran her name. Both were persons of interest in a quadruple homicide. They quickly alerted Durham.

Franklin had already been to Baltimore. Cat had her magazines forwarded. He went to the address. He found out about the death of her baby. The old woman next door confirmed the picture of Vee. He went to the hospital. From there, the lead went cold. It had just gotten red hot.

A day later, he was waiting in the interrogation room for Cat to be brought in. When she entered, his heart dropped. She was nothing like the girl he remembered in high school. She had shriveled and looked ashen. That girl he had a crush on so long ago had been dulled like a rusted jewel. She was the reason why it had become personal for Franklin.

Cat was irritable. She had the runs. Withdrawals were kicking in. The county jail had issued her methadone, but it was a poor substitute for the real thing.

"Hello, Ms. Richards, I'm Detective—"

"I don't give a fuck who you is! Why are ya'll holdin' me?!" she fired at him, pacing the floor.

"I'm sorry for your inconvenience. They were—"

"You shouldn't be able to do this shit if I ain't under arrest!" she huffed.

"True, and the sooner we get this over with, the sooner you can go," he assured her. "Now, please … have a seat."

She folded her arms, eyed him, and finally sat down.

"Like I was sayin', I am Detective Michael Franklin.

Actually, you and I went to high school together. I don't know if you remember me or not," he said hoping she did.

"Oh, is that what this is, a class reunion?" she asked sarcastically.

He smiled and scratched his eyebrow.

"Well, no. I was just—never mind. What can you tell me about Victor Murphy?"

"What do you want to know?"

"Can you tell me where he is?"

"Maybe."

"Maybe?" he echoed.

"Maybe. Depends on what's in it for me," she shot back, scratching her neck.

Now that she knew he had come all the way from Durham, her mind told her to milk it for all it was worth.

Franklin leaned back in the chair.

"A chance to leave, a chance not to be charged with obstruction of justice if I find out you're concealing information."

Cat waived her hand dismissively.

"You already said I could leave, and you won't find out anything I don't want you to. I can find Vee. I'm the only one that can find Vee, trust. You help me and I'll help you," she said, then licked her ashy lips suggestively and put her bony hand on Franklin's.

He withdrew it with contempt.

"Help you how?"

"That depends on one question," she smiled and leaned forward over the table. "How bad you want Vee?"

Ten minutes later, Cat was released. Five minutes

after that, Franklin picked her up around the corner and she showed him the way to her favorite dope spot in Park Heights.

⚫⚫⚫⚫⚫⚫

"Hey, cuzzo!"

"You had us scared for a minute!"

Asia and Brooklyn came to the hospital in Laredo to check on Ty. Part of it was genuine concern and the other was business. Ty had been hit seven times and had died once on the way to the hospital. After two operations he had finally pulled through. The doctors were optimistic that he would walk again, but they knew it would be an uphill battle.

The first thing Ty felt when he woke up was remorse. Like Tito and Vee, he too felt like the hit wouldn't have gone down without Guy's approval. He couldn't blame him. Ty thought Vee had told Guy about Debra's plot and Ty's involvement, and as a result, Guy had let the dogs loose. In a way, Ty felt relief. He no longer had to harbor the guilt. He knew he had been dead wrong, but to protect his mother he would've done it again. But Guy had raised him as his own and this was how he repaid him? Guy's wrath he could accept.

Vee was a different story.

Having nothing to do but think, he knew there was no way for Hardy to have ambushed his people at Karrin's apartment if Vee hadn't pulled his coat to it. That's why Hardy had stopped bringing it to him and just waited on Ty to come to him. It was a strategy he had taught Vee, and now Vee had used it on him.

"Never send a bunch of pussies to do a man's job,"

Ty spat, raising the bed with the remote.

"No doubt, but in certain cases," Brooklyn said, winking at Ty.

He chuckled until it hurt because he knew these pussies could do a man's job.

"On the real, cuzzo, I'm glad to see you. Shit been crazy," Asia remarked, shaking her head.

"And it's about to get crazier," Ty said. "On some real shit, that nigguh Vee caught me slippin', but he fucked up, but I promise you I won't!"

"Yeah, Ty, that's kinda what we wanna talk to you about," Asia began, glancing at Brooklyn.

"What up?"

"We ain't gotta tell you nothin'. Like, this could've happened to you if your father hadn't allowed it," Brooklyn stated.

Ty dropped his head.

"Yeah ... I know."

"But you — something happened to your father."

Ty's heart felt like a lump in his stomach. Brooklyn's tone said it all. His eyes asked what happened.

"Guy got killed, Ty. Aunt Glo killed him, then killed herself," Asia said.

Ty lifted his head, shook it, then slammed it back against the pillow.

"I'm sorry, Ty," Brooklyn said, hugging him.

She was truly sorry that Ty had lost his father, but she was happy that his father had lost his life.

"Why?" he asked, looking from face to face.

Asia shook her head.

"No one knows," she lied. "Sometimes a woman gets fed up."

It was an answer Ty could accept. He knew all the bullshit Guy had put her through over the years. Most of it because of his mother.

"But that's not all," Asia said. "We think Vee callin' the shots now."

"What?!" his anger roared past his tears. "What the fuck you mean?! How?!"

"I don't know, but some nigguhs is respectin' it. We ain't. Tito says to tell you to rest, get well. And when you ready, it's one hundred across the board, whatever you need to take what's yours," Asia assured him.

Asia's words triggered a memory of one of Guy's jewels.

A man only wants a partner for one of two reasons. Either he's weaker and he needs a protector. Or he's stronger and thinks he can swallow you.

Ty knew Tito's offer was based on the second reason. Ty knew if it was Tito's power he used to back the Simmons family for Ty, it would be Tito's power he used to take the Simmons family from Ty. Ty had no intention of being caught slipping twice. He decided to play dead—literally.

"Who knows how I am?" Who knows I'm alive?"

"Just us."

"Keep it that way. A wise man once said you can't stop what you can't see. Let me stay invisible.

Asia nodded understandingly. Cuzzo was back.

●●●●●●

Tito Bell had lived up to his father's legacy and then some. In the streets, his name was loved, feared and respected, not necessarily in that order. He had a vast network of distributors, smugglers, drug houses, and hit teams all over the East Coast, from Boston to Maryland, and as far West as Cleveland, Ohio. In some places they were full-service drug clock, in others strictly weight dealers and some a mixture of the two.

But that wasn't it. He was also heavy in the music game. Sarducci had introduced him to Tommy Mottola, and Tommy helped Tito get a distribution deal for a small urban label he had just received as payment for a drug debt. It had a small stable of artists that Tito made a heavyweight in Hip Hop and R&B.

He had feet planted in two worlds. His artists won Grammys while his dealers controlled the price per gram. He put out hits. Some went platinum and some went to the morgue. Tito was on top of his game.

It was nowhere to go but down.

First it was Cleveland. Major bust, 23 indictments. Over 80 kilos seized. Then three months later Bridgeport, Connecticut, which dominoed into Waterbury and Hartford. Wilmington, Delaware fell soon after. It was like he was being boxed in. He just didn't know it was being orchestrated by Guy.

"Ay, yo, Tito, nigguh named Jerome from Morningside say he wanna holla at you my dude," the bouncer told Tito.

Tito was in the V.I.P. section of the famous Cheetah's in Manhattan with Steve Stout and Lyor Cohen when the bouncer approached. Tito smiled to himself. A lot had changed since he had last seen Jerome. He couldn't help but show his childhood rival who was the man now. Besides, Tito respected Jerome's hustle. He knew he was just coming home from doing twelve in the Feds after being bagged in Charlestown, West Virginia with a brick and a half. Jerome had held his weight, keeping his name good in the streets.

But the streets didn't know what happened after he got out. Most dudes turn rat not to go to prison or to get out or prison. Jerome turned rat when he came home. Finding himself twelve years behind the game, broke, and without a break, the Feds offered to turn a blind eye to what he did and what they'd help him do if he worked for them.

He took the deal. The Feds gave him to Guy in exchange for Cleveland. Guy pointed Jerome in Tito's direction. He became Guy's mole in the Bell organization. It was Guy's idea spoken through Jerome's mouth that made Tito consider a move down South and an alliance with the Simmonses. Tito only thought it was his idea. Which was exactly what Guy wanted him to think.

"Tito, what up, my nigguh! Long time no see!" Jerome exclaimed, giving Tito a full hug.

Tito accepted it and embraced him.

"What up, Rome? You ain't lookin' too bad yourself," Tito complimented.

Jerome's watch and pinky ring were no way Tito status, but they said Jerome had been busy since his rebirth to redefine himself for the new millennium.

"I can dig it, Silk," Tito laughed.

The conversation ventured back in the day, the game then and the game now.

"I'm tellin' you, my nigguh, the game down South is sweet! VA, down NC, ATL. Shit, a nigguh can feast, but I can't get a connect worth a fuck," Jerome said.

Tito read in between the lines, but played it nonchalantly.

"Good people hard to find these days."

"Not if you know where to look."

"Shit used to be about thoroughbreds. Now it's about just keepin' your horse out the glue factory."

"I always ran with thoroughbreds. You know my pedigree," Silk boasted.

"True indeed," Tito acknowledged, then shrugged, "I don't know, Rome — I mean, Silk … let me holla at some people. Down South don't sound like a bad idea," Tito said, thinking of his Uncle Guy, formulating a plan in that quick mind of his.

Satisfied, Silk extended his hand.

"That's what it is then, my nigguh. Get at me."

Tito had Silk checked out and he came back solid. He planned on using him as his scout into the South and ultimately into the Simmons network. He just didn't know Guy had thought of using Silk first.

Then Queens happened.

It wasn't a large bust in terms of product or money, but it was the beginning of subtle distancing between Sarducci and Tito. Neither knew the invisible enemy was to blame.

"You know the worst kind of enemy, Tito?" Sarducci had asked one day over one of his dinners.

"The kind you can't see," Tito replied with hesitation.

Sarducci smiled. Tito had come a long way.

"Exactly. It's worse than a friend turned enemy because this invisible enemy is just a nameless, faceless — it's almost like havin' God against ya' 'cause he strikes without a warnin'," Sarducci joked.

Tito saw his point and chuckled, although the situation was no laughing matter. In Cleveland, it was the Feds. In Connecticut, the DEA. In Delaware, ATF. Sarducci blamed it on the fact that Tito's organization was too big and was getting sloppy. Tito saw the whole picture. It was too systematic to be random. His street instincts sensed something bigger, and he felt only Sarducci was big enough to have an enemy of that magnitude.

"Whatever the reason," Tre said, taking the hint.

"It's a wrap, my nigguh," Tre had told Tito.

Tre and Sleep had set up in Baltimore. They were moving cocaine and heroin. But once things began to fall apart, Tre bowed out gracefully.

"I'm tellin' you, Tito, we had a hell of a run. Most dudes don't even see half as long a run. Ride with me on this," Tre had urged.

"I love you like a brother, fam, but believe me, after this move I got planned, then we can fall back," Tito replied, thinking of his plan to expand into the South.

"Do you, my nigguh, but me and Sleep 'bout to move on this porn shit. It's a billion-dollar industry!"

"Let me find out ya'll about to be male strippers gone wild!" Tito laughed.

Tre laughed too.

"Nigguh, fuck you! Just watch, I'ma be the black Hugh Hefner!"

The conversation with Tre was on his mind a few weeks later, at the family reunion in Aruba. He had personally asked Guy to come.

"Come down to Aruba, Unk. Relax, it's the Bells," Tito had offered.

But when he looked and saw his Aunt Gloria arrive, she was only accompanied by Kev and Ty. He smiled when he saw them, comfortable in their own swag and all grown up. But that smiled faded when he realized Guy wasn't coming. That was a bad sign, but at least he had sent Kev and Ty.

Boy I need you as bad as my heartbeat
Bad like the food I eat
Bad as the air I breathe
Baby I want you bad

Jazmine Sullivan sang as Tito made his way through the crowd. He came over to his mother, Gloria, Ty, and Kev just in time to hear Kev say, "Aunt T, um ...where's Tito?"

"Oh, he should be – "

"Right here," Tito finished for her, hugging his Aunt Gloria, then his cousins. "Glad to see ya'll could make it, "Tito greeted.

"And miss a free trip to Aruba? Boy, bye," Gloria chuckled.

"What up, Kev? It's been a minute. Let's find somewhere to talk. We got a lot of catchin' up to do."

CHAPTER 49

Guy Simmons was gone.

His run had extended four decades, a stretch rarely achieved in the game. He fought dirty. If you crossed him, death was a mercy.

In the end, he had gained the world, but lost what truly mattered to him: his family. Now all that was left was the one man who had destroyed it all, the same one who was now asked to rebuild it: Vee.

He stood beside his mother, who sat in the place of the grieving widow. As the tears streamed down her face, she remembered her own words as a young girl: "Nigguh, I am your wife!"

She loved Guy, but when she had walked out, she had let go. His death was painful, but she exhaled the last of Guy. Therefore, she had her own air to sustain her.

On the other side of Vee was Willie in his wheelchair. Hawk Bill was beside him. The four of them were enveloped in a semi-circle of bodyguards.

Across from the grave, Tito stood with Asia and Brooklyn.

As the preacher elegantly eulogized the Guy Simmons the outside world knew, Vee and Tito locked eyes over the coffin. Tito wore sunglasses. Vee didn't. Both gazes said they were extremely confident and that the other man was the lesser. Like two boxers, both wore belts, both were undefeated, looking to unify the title.

When the service concluded, the bell rang.

"Ma, you okay?" Vee asked, hugging Shantelle and kissing her on her cheek.

She nodded, dabbed her eyes, and mustered a smile. "I will be."

"What he doin' here?" Willie gruffed, glaring at Tito.

"I'm about to find out," Vee assured him.

Hawk Bill pushed Willie away with Shantelle on his arm.

Tito, Asia, and Brooklyn approached Vee.

"My condolences for you … loss," Tito remarked, making sure the meaning of the pause wasn't missed.

He extended his hand.

Vee disregarded it.

"You can't rock me to sleep, Tito."

Tito shrugged, smirked, then put his hand in his pocket.

"Then instead of condolences, congratulations. I guess you the man, little cuz."

"You lied to me yo," Vee accused.

"How you figure that?"

"You told me you and Tre would stay neutral, but then you let Ty use the studio for his jump off. Now, if you say you ain't have nothin' to do wit' that, then maybe you ain't in charge like you say you are, but if you are in charge, then you're a liar," Vee reasoned smoothly.

Tito nodded and rocked nonchalantly on his heels.

"Okay. I feel you. But I didn't come here for a problem. I came here hoping to solve 'em. I mean, look around you. No, really … look around you."

Vee didn't need to. He had already seen the subtle placing of Tito's team all around the perimeter of the cemetery. If he wanted to, Tito could've massacred the whole funeral. Guy's team was dispersed haphazardly and half asleep to the setup.

"If I wanted war, all I'd have to do is nod," Tito grinned. "But I'm not. All I'm sayin' is Guy and I had a deal on the table. I'm just asking you to honor it. Actually, it was Ty's deal. But since Ty's dead," Tito lied, "it's in your lap."

"I'm not Guy," Vee replied simply, then began to turn away.

"Listen, I know your head's all fucked up right now, so I'ma give you a chance to think about this. Then you can get back to me," Tito offered calmly but with an undertone of steel.

"Yeah … I'll get at you," Vee smirked, his words meaning the exact opposite.

Tito caught it, but let it go. He and Asia walked away, but Brooklyn stepped up to Vee.

"You and I almost met once," she began, thinking of that night at his apartment. "It would be a shame for us to meet again."

"Naw, ma, I look forward to it. And bring your stutter," Vee replied, referring to her twin.

Brooklyn laughed as he walked away.

"I like you. This is going to be fun."

Vee was heated. He hated to be caught slipping. Guy's team was a joke. They were definitely killers, but it had been so long since they had been battle tested, they had grown lazy. Vee planned on dealing with that ASAP.

As he walked towards the line of limos, a woman parked three limos down from his stepped out of hers.

She was wearing very a conservative black dress, but to Vee, despite what she wore, her energy was naked underneath. Her beauty was an expression of sensuality and strength, a combination that could break any man's heart. Vee just didn't have one.

"Hello, Victor. I … um … just came to convey my sincerest condolences," Vanya began, fighting down the fluster she felt when she was in Vee's presence.

What does this man do to me, she thought to herself.

"Thank you."

"I hope you don't think I'm disrespectful for coming here to see you. I've been calling you, but you haven't returned my calls."

"I don't answer numbers I don't know," Vee answered, maintaining an emotional distance.

"Texts that say 'This is Vanya' too?" she chuckled.

"Look, I ain't with Red Light and your boy Tito no more, so I figured what's the point.

Vanya smiled understandingly. Now it made more sense. Vee thought that Vanya was connected to Tito, and because what transpired between them in Baltimore involved bullets, she represented the enemy to Vee.

"Trust me, Victor, Tito is definitely not the point. Don't get me wrong, he is a beautiful brother, one I admire and respect, but Tito knows I'd eat him for breakfast. Not in a gangsta way, but in my own way, which would be just as effective. I have no strings attached to my intentions," Vanya explained, breaking it down to Vee.

He couldn't help but feel relief. There was no denying their chemistry, but ...

"I respect that, but shit is hectic right now and I—"

"I don't believe in bad timing," she said, cutting him off. "That's as silly as believing in destiny. But I can see where this is heading. Three strong black men ready to give up their future for the past. As your sister, I implore you to open your eyes. But as a woman, I want to help you."

Vee had never met a woman like Vanya. Her presence made him smile.

"Help me? What makes you think you can?"

She cocked her head at a flirtatious angle and smiled.

"Because I am a goddess, my every wish must be obeyed."

Persistence overcomes resistance.

Vee laughed.

"Now, take me to meet your mother so I can thank her," Vanya quipped as she brushed past Vee and headed for his limo.

❂❂❂❂❂❂❂

Back at the ranch, members of the Simmons and Braswell families, friends, and acquaintances mingled, ate, mourned, and drank the plentiful free liquor.

Vee felt like an outsider, although technically he was the host. The house was full of strangers mourning a stranger, and like Pac said, "My anger wouldn't let me feel for a stranger."

He left Vanya and his mother together while he went outside. He walked up to Hawk Bill.

"Man, damn, I can't believe the ol' boy is gone," Hawk Bill said, shaking his head and downing his drink. "I'ma miss that mule-headed sum' bitch."

Vee surveyed the scenery.

"He was slippin', Unk. Look at this shit. Me and my Wolf Pack nigguhs could've come through and laid the whole place down. Just six of us, yo," Vee remarked with disgust, looking at how Guy's security was set up.

Hawk Bill shrugged.

"Who the hell was gonna test Guy Simmons? Back in the day, it woulda been a suicide mission. His team was the best. Now they ain't worth a goddamn," Hawk Bill agreed.

"You need to do something about it," Vee said.

"Me? Seem like you in a better position to handle it," Hawk Bill replied.

Vee didn't answer. He still hadn't accepted what life seemed to be forcing him to accept. Ever since Kev had Pappy and Rico killed and brought him into this whole thing, Vee had been moving like his hand had been forced. Every move had been defensive. Vee had yet to take the offensive.

Now his main concern was Kev's seed. Not because of guilt or sense of duty, but because of self-preservation. His dreams didn't lie, and his dream told him to protect the seed. Everything else was irrelevant. It would be Willie who convinced him otherwise.

"Get in," Willie gruffed from the back of the limo.

He pulled up in front of Vee and Hawk Bill. Vee looked at Hawk Bill.

"Not him, you. Come on heah," Willie ordered as if no wasn't an option, then opened the door.

"Where we goin'?"

"Whereva I take ya'," Willie retorted impatiently. "Now get cheah. I ain't sayin' it no goddamn mo'."

Miss Sadie made Vee respect his elders, so he bit his tongue and got in the limo.

Willie took him to his farm on the outskirts of Goldsboro. An older white couple and their kids ran the farm for Willie, never knowing what they were really a front for.

And on this farm, Willie kept a liquor still, one of the first ones ever made. It was in top shape. Willie had Vee push his wheelchair to liquor still, inside a small barn.

"You know what this is?"

"Nah."

"It's a still. Make co'n liquor with it," Willie explained.

"Make what with it?" Vee repeated, still not used to the geechie in Willie's drawl.

"Co'n liquor, co'n liquor! Country-ass nigguh," Willie chuckled, having the audacity to call somebody else country. "You ever drunk of it?"

Vee shook his head.

"Well you fittin' to," Willie told him.

He pulled out his flask, then filled it from the top of the still. He took a big gulp, then made the ugly face.

"Whoo! Goddamn right! One sip o' this make the pastor preach all day!" Willie laughed, then held it out to Vee. "Hmph!"

"I'm good."

"Nigguh, I said hmph! You too good to drink wit' yo' grandfolk?"

Their eyes met and Vee realized what he was offering was much more than a drink. Vee took a sip.

"Boy, is ya' prissy? Drink that goddamn shit!"

Vee threw his head back. When he brought it down, he was already tipsy.

"See that? Best co'n liquor in bot' Carolinas. Recipe been in our family since slavery. But each generation dem add something to it. Make 'em better. That what us heah about. The Simmons. And that ain't no white man name none! You bunch o' great grandfolk him a horse thief. When they catch 'em deah, them say, 'Boy, what you name is?' He say seaman 'cause he come from nether Gullah Islands, from the sea. But him talk them white men can't understand, sound like Simmons. That theah our name," Willie explained, taking the flask and hitting it again.

Vee didn't know if it was the buzz or the words, but he felt a strong pride knowing he came from a man who refused to be a slave or bear any other name but his own.

"Fo' yo' diddy, nan' Simmons could read. Readin' for dem uppity niggahs got the guns. You bet' not forget you a nigguh! Your diddy wanted to fo'get him a niggauh, but I made him be one."

Willie dropped his head and the tears dropped off his leathery cheeks.

Vee had never seen a man cry. He was stuck. Willie recovered after only a few tears.

"I was scared. Scared of him not be a nigguh. What him then? Nothin'! And the only thing worse than bein' a nigguh is bein' nothin'. But him go and see the world. It full of nigguhs! He came back a nigguh, and he make Kev a nigguh and you a nigguh and Ty. And I tell you, Ty ain't no Simmons. Him Hardy. Guy no him diddy!"

Vee nodded like he expected it. Like in the back of his mind, he sensed it.

"Now, I didn't blame you fo' what happened. I blame me! But we can't change that theah. But I need you, boy. I swear fo' God and fo' mo' white folks I need you! That baby deah ... don't let that baby be no nigguh," Willie roared. Vee felt it in his spine.

Willie held on until he got it all out. Now he wept uncontrollably. It was the closest Vee had ever come to shedding a tear. He could feel his grandfather's pain. In trying to protect his son, he had condemned him, just like Vee did with Taheem. The road to hell is paved with good intentions.

Vee laid his hand on his grandfather's shoulder.

"I won't."

Do the ends justify the means?

That was the recurring question in Franklin's head as he looked at the flier Karrin had made in her search for Cat. She used her high-school graduation picture. The way Franklin remembered her. The cattish slant to her eyes that gave Cat her nickname and made every expression so alluring. The way her hair always seemed to fall over her left eye reminded him of Aaliyah. He lowered the picture and looked at her in a dope nod on his couch. It was like before and after. She was only a skeleton of her former self, but when she appeared sleep, in a nod, the fiend of addiction dissolved and left that serene beauty common to sleeping babies. Besides, as his eyes wandered down the length of her body to her gym-short clad legs, he could see that she hadn't lost her shapeliness, courtesy of running track in high school.

"Every closed eye ain't sleep Franklin," Cat teased him in the scraggly voice of a dope fiend, lifting her head slightly.

Embarrassed, Franklin changed the conversation.

"Kianna, it's been three days, and you still haven't made good on your end of the deal. Today's the deadline," he told her firmly.

"You see I'm tryin'," she whined. "Those posters are all over Bmore. Believe me, they'll answer."

"Deadline, Kianna," Franklin repeated. "Or I promise you, I'll put you back on the streets."

Cat could tell by the tone of his voice he was dead serious. She had spent the last three days trying every emotional trick in an addict's book—cajoling, begging, guilt trips, temper tantrums—to keep him supplying her with drugs before she found Vee.

Franklin had justified it as medicine. Keeping her from being sick so he could solve the murders. He had come to rely on Silk more and more, a fact that Silk hadn't let him miss.

"We brothers in the same struggle, huh Frank?" Silk had said, handing Franklin the bundle of dope.

He snatched it out his hand.

"Just gimme this garbage," Franklin seethed and pulled off.

Franklin tossed his phone at her. It landed in her lap. "Now."

Cat could've been called Red Light Studios, but she thought after she turned Vee in, her free ride was over. But she knew she had to do something.

She Googled Red Light on his phone and made the call.

"Red Light Studios," a woman answered.

"I need to speak with Tre."

"Who is it?" she asked.

"Cat, Vee's baby mama."

"Hold please."

When Tre heard who was calling for him, he felt like the universe was smiling on him. The deal with Vanya seemed to be hanging by a string, and that string was Vee. But Vee wouldn't return Tre's calls or texts. Tre's pride wanted to say fuck that nigguh, but he swallowed it because of the deal.

He knew if anybody could get at Vee, it was Cat.

"What's up, ma? What's good?" Tre greeted her cheerfully.

"I need to speak to Vee," she replied in a firm tone.

"Shit, ma, I do too," he chuckled. "Unfortunately, I can't seem to reach the nigguh. Maybe you'll have better luck. His math is 302-555-3341. And tell my nigguh I got that money for him so to hit me ASAP!" Tre offered, trying to give Vee an incentive.

"I'll tell him," Cat lied.

"Where can I reach you?"

"You can't."

Click.

She hung up and looked at Franklin. "302-555-3341," she said with attitude, then tossed his phone back at him.

"You could've done that from jump," Franklin spat frustratedly.

"Oh, well, you got it now, don't you?"

He tossed the phone at her harder. It hit her in the chest. She drew back to throw it.

"I wish the fu—" He caught himself and said, "Just call him."

Cat smacked her teeth but she complied.

Three days after Guy was buried, Karrin gave birth to an 8-pound, 3-ounce baby boy. She named him Travon.

She sat in the hospital bed, holding the feisty little boy. Vee closed the door behind him.

"You want to hold him?" Karrin offered with a smile.

"No," Vee replied without one.

She could tell Vee wasn't there for small talk, so she attempted to plead her case.

"What do you think Cat would've done if it had been you? Do you expect her love for you to have been any less? Doesn't that count for something? If not for me, then for the baby, Vee. We, you and I, are all he has in this world. I may deserve your hatred, but Travon doesn't. If nothing else, think about that."

"Finished?"

Karrin dropped her head because she could see her words fell on deaf ears. When she didn't respond, Vee said, "You gonna give us custody of the baby, in the name of Shantelle Braswell. You can have visitation, but only supervised. In return, you get to keep breathin'. Are we clear?"

"No."

"No, you don't want to live, or no, you don't want to die?" Vee shot back.

"No, I will not give up custody of my child. Travon will stay with me, and I will stay with this family, and we both will be taken care of. If anything happens to me, my parents and Cat's parents will know who to hold accountable. Now, are we clear?" Karrin countered with more confidence than she really felt.

She put Cat's parents in it in an attempt to use Vee's love for Cat against him.

Karrin had overplayed her hand.

Vee smiled coldly. She liked it better when he scowled. He approached, got close to her ear, and replied, "Then I will kill your mother and father and her mother and father. I will do it slow. It will be painful. And I will make you watch," he hissed sincerely. Then he added with less intensity, "Then I will put a gun in your hand and make you choose between you and this goddamn bastard, and we'll see how much you really care for your baby," he lied.

The chill Karrin felt was communicated by energy to the baby because he began to scream at the top of his lungs. By the time Vee was finished, Karrin was in tears.

"Please, Vee, please. Don't do this! Don't take my baby from me! He's all I got! Kev's gone and Ty's gone! I ain't got nothin'! Please, Vee, don't do this! What am I going to do?!" she cried.

"Exactly what I say," he answered calmly.

"Please ..."

He paused at the door.

"And yo, change his name. Change it to Guy Simmons."

Then he walked out.

As Vee drove from the hospital, he received two texts back to back. One from the present and one from the past. Vanya and Cat.

Vanya's text read:
I want to see you.

Cat's text read:
I need to see you.

There was no way Vee would ignore Cat. Even though his gut was telling him no, his love for Cat made him say yes, and he did what he never did before: He went against his instincts.

"Cat?" he said when she picked up. "Where you at?"

"B-b-baby, I need you," she sobbed. "I'm so sorry about everything, but I need you, Vee."

"I'm on my way. Don't worry. I got you," Vee vowed.

"O-okay. I-I'm in the shelter. Downtown. I love you, Vee."

"Yeah. Yeah, I love you too," Vee replied after a moment of hesitation. Then he hung up.

As soon as she broke the connection, Cat's crocodile tears dried up.

"Happy now?" she asked, handing Franklin back the phone.

Franklin just looked at Cat. He wasn't surprised by the things a woman could fake. He was surprised that despite a woman's ability to deceive, there was one thing they couldn't fake: their love.

"What?" Cat smirked, watching him watch her. "This? A woman can fake a lot of things."

"Not everything," he replied.

Her eyes said she knew what he was talking about, but she didn't respond. Franklin phoned in and set up the perimeter around the homeless shelter on West Pettigrew Street.

When he hung up, Cat asked, "What's going to happen to me now?"

"What do you mean?" Franklin inquired, playing stupid.

"You've got what you wanted. What do you need me for?" she replied using her tone to try and invoke pity.

"That depends on you."

"How?"

He looked her in her eyes.

"No more games, Kianna. But only if you play it straight, you understand?"

She nodded, but her agile mind was already trying to find an angle to play.

"Let's go."

Vee hadn't even considered the fact that he was going to Durham until he actually came off the exit for West Pettigrew. Then it hit him. He was a wanted man. The thought didn't worry him; it just made his gut resist that much more. Something's wrong!

But he couldn't turn back. Whatever it was, Vee had to come. After all they had been through, after all he had put her through, Vee felt like he owed her at least this, whatever it cost him. Guilt is more powerful when it wears the mask of love. That was the mistake Vee made. He had come because of guilt, not because of love. He hadn't realized his love died the day in the dressing room, when Cat chose another man over him.

Vee pulled up across the street from the shelter. Cat was standing outside, waiting.

"No one move until I say," Franklin reaffirmed through his headset.

He was positioned in the store beside the shelter, watching.

Vee got out. He and Cat looked at each other. She didn't move. Didn't crack a smile. His gut raged. He started to cross the street but someone honked a car horn. He looked in that direction. That's when he saw two unmarked cars parked in the adjacent parking lot to block his west side. He automatically looked to the right. Another unmarked to block his east side. He and the driver locked eyes. Vee smiled.

"Go! Go! We're blown! Move in!"

Those were the words Franklin heard over his headset. The team was jumping the gun.

"No! No! Do not—" Franklin began, but it was too late.

All he heard was accelerating engines, screeching tires, and slamming doors. He snatched open the store's door, gun drawn.

In that split second of realization, Vee could've gotten away. The alley directly behind him was uncovered because it looked like a dead end. It wasn't and Vee knew it. Instead, he looked at Cat. He stopped in the middle of the street and held his arms open, inviting an embrace, the mockery of a smile on his face.

Franklin aimed his gun at Vee and yelled, "Freeze!" But he too recognized that Vee could've tried to get away but didn't.

"Don't move, Victor. No need to get ugly," Franklin warned, keeping his gun poised while another officer ran up to cuff him. Vee didn't even acknowledge his presence. His eyes never left Cat.

Her posture conveyed strength. She held her head up and stared straight at him. Vindication. Hadn't Vee taken everything from her? Now she would take everything from him. Vindication was the single tear that dropped from her eye.

As his rights were read to him, Vee thought about Cat's words in his dream: Nothin' except love …

●●●●●●

"Don't worry, lil' cuz, we gonna take good care of you. Surround you with the best doctors and the baddest bitches. You'll be on your feet in no time — unless it'll be more fun to be on your back," Tito joked. Tito, his two shooters, Brooklyn, and Asia all laughed.

They had come to pick Ty up from the hospital. The whole scene had a family feel, but underneath no one's motives were familial.

Franklin and four county sheriffs stepped up and blocked their path.

"Hello, Ty. Glad to see you pulled through," Franklin quipped with a grin that said, I got you.

Finding Ty was easy. He was in the hospital under his real name. When Franklin put in his name, Montgomery County, MD came back.

There rest was just a matter of logistics.

"Yo, Ty, who is this clown?" Tito spat with disgust.

"Clown? No, I'm Detective Franklin, Durham County Police. And you are?"

"A nigguh you don't want to fuck wit," Tito shot coldly.

Franklin snickered and nodded.

"I'll keep that in mind," he replied. "I think we've got him from here."

One of the officers moved to get the wheelchair. Tito reluctantly let go.

"What the fuck is this about, Franklin? You arrestin' me?!" Ty barked.

"Oh, my bad. I was so excited to see you, I forgot. Tyquan Simmons, you're under arrest for first-degree murder," Franklin informed him.

"Murder?" Asia echoed.

"Ty, what's up?" Tito probed.

"Fuck this nigguh, yo. It's nothin'. I'll be out before we get back to Durham," Ty bragged arrogantly.

One of the officers read him his rights. The Bells watched them go out the automatic doors.

"Shit!" Tito swore.

Outside, as they prepared to load Ty into the sheriff's van, Franklin turned to him and asked, "Do you think I look like Wayne Brady? Because a lot of people say I look like Will Smith, but I think I look more like Wayne Brady."

Ty was vexed and didn't want to talk, but the

comment was so left field, human curiosity got the best of him.

"Who the fuck is Wayne Brady?"

Franklin smiled. "You know, the black guy from 'Let's Make a Deal.'"

Ty looked at Franklin. He got his point. He was offering him a way out ...

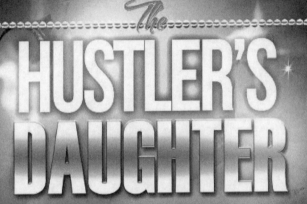

The
HUSTLER'S
DAUGHTER

BY
PINKY
DIOR

A BEAUTIFUL SATAN II

NATASHA'S WRATH

By RJ CHAMP

Order Form

DC Bookdiva Publications
#245 4401-A Connecticut Avenue, NW
Washington, DC 20008
dcbookdiva.com

Name: _____
InmateID: ____ _____
Address: _____
City/State: _____ **Zip:** _____

QUANTITY	TITLES	PRICE	TOTAL
	Up The Way, Ben	15.00	
	Dynasty By Dutch	15.00	
	Dynasty 2 By Dutch	15.00	
	Trina, Darrell Debrew	15.00	
	A Killer'z Ambition, Nathan Welch	15.00	
	Lorton Legends, Eyone Williams	15.00	
	The Hustle. Frazier Boy	15.00	
	A Beautiful Satan, RJ Champ	15.00	
	Secrets Never Die, Eyone Williams	15.00	
	Q, Dutch	15.00	

QUANTITY	TITLES	PRICE	TOTAL
	Dynasty 3, Dutch	15.00	
	Tina, Darrell Debrew	15.00	
	A Beautiful Satan 2, RJ Champ	15.00	
	A Hustler's Daughter, Pinky Dior	15.00	
	A Killer'z Ambition 2, Nathan Welch	15.00	
	The Commission	15.00	

Sub-Total $_____

Shipping/Handling (Via US Media Mail) $3.95 1-2 Books, $7.95 1-3 Books, 4 or more titles-Free Shipping

Shipping $ ____ _____
Total Enclosed $_____

Certified or government issued checks and money orders, all mail in orders take 5-7 Business days to be delivered. Books can also be purchased on our website at dcbookdiva.com and by credit card at 1866-928-9990. Incarcerated readers receive 25% discount. Please pay $11.25 per book and apply the same shipping terms as stated above.